THE PELICAN SHAKESPEARE

GENERAL EDITOR ALFRED HARBAGE

THE TRAGEDY OF

KING RICHARD THE THIRD

WILLIAM SHAKESPEARE

THE TRAGEDY OF KING RICHARD THE THIRD

EDITED BY G. BLAKEMORE EVANS

PENGUIN BOOKS

Penguin Books Ltd, Harmondsworth,
Middlesex, England
Penguin Books, 625 Madison Avenue,
New York, New York 10022, U.S.A.
Penguin Books Australia Ltd, Ringwood,
Victoria, Australia
Penguin Books Canada Limited, 2801 John Street,
Markham, Ontario, Canada L3R 1B4
Penguin Books (N.Z.) Ltd, 182–190 Wairau Road,
Auckland 10, New Zealand

First published in *The Pelican Shakespeare* 1959
This revised edition first published 1969
Reprinted 1973, 1974, 1978, 1979, 1980

Library of Congress catalog card number: 79-95580

Printed in the United States of America by
Kingsport Press, Inc., Kingsport, Tennessee
Set in Monotype Ehrhardt

CONTENTS

PUBLISHER'S NOTE

Soon after the thirty-eight volumes forming *The Pelican Shakespeare* had been published, they were brought together in *The Complete Pelican Shakespeare*. The editorial revisions and new textual features are explained in detail in the General Editor's Preface to the one-volume edition. They have all been incorporated in the present volume. The following should be mentioned in particular:

The lines are not numbered in arbitrary units. Instead all lines are numbered which contain a word, phrase, or allusion explained in the glossarial notes. In the occasional instances where there is a long stretch of unannotated text, certain lines are numbered in italics to serve the conventional reference purpose.

The intrusive and often inaccurate place-headings inserted by early editors are omitted (as is becoming standard practise), but for the convenience of those who miss them, an indication of locale now appears as first item in the annotation of each scene.

In the interest of both elegance and utility, each speech-prefix is set in a separate line when the speaker's lines are in verse, except when these words form the second half of a pentameter line. Thus the verse form of the speech is kept visually intact, and turned-over lines are avoided. What is printed as verse and what is printed as prose has, in general, the authority of the original texts. Departures from the original texts in this regard have only the authority of editorial tradition and the judgment of the Pelican editors; and, in a few instances, are admittedly arbitrary.

SHAKESPEARE AND
HIS STAGE

William Shakespeare was christened in Holy Trinity
Church, Stratford-upon-Avon, April 26, 1564. His birth
is traditionally assigned to April 23. He was the eldest of
four boys and two girls who survived infancy in the family
of John Shakespeare, glover and trader of Henley Street,
and his wife Mary Arden, daughter of a small landowner
of Wilmcote. In 1568 John was elected Bailiff (equivalent
to Mayor) of Stratford, having already filled the minor
municipal offices. The town maintained for the sons of the
burgesses a free school, taught by a university graduate
and offering preparation in Latin sufficient for university
entrance; its early registers are lost, but there can be little
doubt that Shakespeare received the formal part of his
education in this school.

On November 27, 1582, a license was issued for the
marriage of William Shakespeare (aged eighteen) and Ann
Hathaway (aged twenty-six), and on May 26, 1583, their
child Susanna was christened in Holy Trinity Church.
The inference that the marriage was forced upon the youth
is natural but not inevitable; betrothal was legally binding
at the time, and was sometimes regarded as conferring
conjugal rights. Two additional children of the marriage,
the twins Hamnet and Judith, were christened on Feb-
ruary 2, 1585. Meanwhile the prosperity of the elder
Shakespeares had declined, and William was impelled to
seek a career outside Stratford.

The tradition that he spent some time as a country

teacher is old but unverifiable. Because of the absence of records his early twenties are called the "lost years," and only one thing about them is certain – that at least some of these years were spent in winning a place in the acting profession. He may have begun as a provincial trouper, but by 1592 he was established in London and prominent enough to be attacked. In a pamphlet of that year, *Groats-worth of Wit*, the ailing Robert Greene complained of the neglect which university writers like himself had suffered from actors, one of whom was daring to set up as a playwright:

... an vpstart Crow, beautified with our feathers, that with his *Tygers hart wrapt in a Players hyde*, supposes he is as well able to bombast out a blanke verse as the best of you: and beeing an absolute *Iohannes fac totum*, is in his owne conceit the onely Shake-scene in a countrey.

The pun on his name, and the parody of his line "O tiger's heart wrapped in a woman's hide" (*3 Henry VI*), pointed clearly to Shakespeare. Some of his admirers protested, and Henry Chettle, the editor of Greene's pamphlet, saw fit to apologize:

... I am as sory as if the originall fault had beene my fault, because my selfe haue seene his demeanor no lesse ciuill than he excelent in the qualitie he professes: Besides, diuers of worship haue reported his vprightnes of dealing, which argues his honesty, and his facetious grace in writting, that approoues his Art. (Prefatory epistle, *Kind-Harts Dreame*)

The plague closed the London theatres for many months in 1592–94, denying the actors their livelihood. To this period belong Shakespeare's two narrative poems, *Venus and Adonis* and *The Rape of Lucrece*, both dedicated to the Earl of Southampton. No doubt the poet was rewarded with a gift of money as usual in such cases, but he did no further dedicating and we have no reliable information on whether Southampton, or anyone else, became his regular patron. His sonnets, first mentioned in 1598 and published without his consent in 1609, are intimate without being

8

explicitly autobiographical. They seem to commemorate the poet's friendship with an idealized youth, rivalry with a more favored poet, and love affair with a dark mistress; and his bitterness when the mistress betrays him in conjunction with the friend; but it is difficult to decide precisely what the "story" is, impossible to decide whether it is fictional or true. The true distinction of the sonnets, at least of those not purely conventional, rests in the universality of the thoughts and moods they express, and in their poignancy and beauty.

In 1594 was formed the theatrical company known until 1603 as the Lord Chamberlain's men, thereafter as the King's men. Its original membership included, besides Shakespeare, the beloved clown Will Kempe and the famous actor Richard Burbage. The company acted in various London theatres and even toured the provinces, but it is chiefly associated in our minds with the Globe Theatre built on the south bank of the Thames in 1599. Shakespeare was an actor and joint owner of this company (and its Globe) through the remainder of his creative years. His plays, written at the average rate of two a year, together with Burbage's acting won it its place of leadership among the London companies.

Individual plays began to appear in print, in editions both honest and piratical, and the publishers became increasingly aware of the value of Shakespeare's name on the title pages. As early as 1598 he was hailed as the leading English dramatist in the *Palladis Tamia* of Francis Meres:

As *Plautus* and *Seneca* are accounted the best for Comedy and Tragedy among the Latines, so *Shakespeare* among the English is the most excellent in both kinds for the stage: for Comedy, witnes his *Gentlemen of Verona*, his *Errors*, his *Loue labors lost*, his *Loue labours wonne* [at one time in print but no longer extant, at least under this title], his *Midsummers night dream*, & his *Merchant of Venice*; for Tragedy, his *Richard the 2*, *Richard the 3*, *Henry the 4*, *King Iohn*, *Titus Andronicus*, and his *Romeo and Iuliet*.

The note is valuable both in indicating Shakespeare's prestige and in helping us to establish a chronology. In the second half of his writing career, history plays gave place to the great tragedies; and farces and light comedies gave place to the problem plays and symbolic romances. In 1623, seven years after his death, his former fellow-actors, John Heminge and Henry Condell, cooperated with a group of London printers in bringing out his plays in collected form. The volume is generally known as the First Folio.

Shakespeare had never severed his relations with Stratford. His wife and children may sometimes have shared his London lodgings, but their home was Stratford. His son Hamnet was buried there in 1596, and his daughters Susanna and Judith were married there in 1607 and 1616 respectively. (His father, for whom he had secured a coat of arms and thus the privilege of writing himself gentleman, died in 1601, his mother in 1608.) His considerable earnings in London, as actor-sharer, part owner of the Globe, and playwright, were invested chiefly in Stratford property. In 1597 he purchased for £60 New Place, one of the two most imposing residences in the town. A number of other business transactions, as well as minor episodes in his career, have left documentary records. By 1611 he was in a position to retire, and he seems gradually to have withdrawn from theatrical activity in order to live in Stratford. In March, 1616, he made a will, leaving token bequests to Burbage, Heminge, and Condell, but the bulk of his estate to his family. The most famous feature of the will, the bequest of the second-best bed to his wife, reveals nothing about Shakespeare's marriage; the quaintness of the provision seems commonplace to those familiar with ancient testaments. Shakespeare died April 23, 1616, and was buried in the Stratford church where he had been christened. Within seven years a monument was erected to his memory on the north wall of the chancel. Its portrait bust and the Droeshout engraving on the title page of the First Folio provide the only likenesses with an established claim to authenticity. The best verbal vignette was written by his rival Ben Jonson, the more impressive for being imbedded in a context mainly critical:

... I loved the man, and doe honour his memory (on this side idolatry) as much as any. Hee was indeed honest, and of an open and free nature: had an excellent Phantsie, brave notions, and gentle expressions.... (*Timber or Discoveries*, ca. 1623–30)

*

The reader of Shakespeare's plays is aided by a general knowledge of the way in which they were staged. The King's men acquired a roofed and artificially lighted theatre only toward the close of Shakespeare's career, and then only for winter use. Nearly all his plays were designed for performance in such structures as the Globe – a three-tiered amphitheatre with a large rectangular platform extending to the center of its yard. The plays were staged by daylight, by large casts brilliantly costumed, but with only a minimum of properties, without scenery, and quite possibly without intermissions. There was a rear stage gallery for action "above," and a curtained rear recess for "discoveries" and other special effects, but by far the major portion of any play was enacted upon the projecting platform, with episode following episode in swift succession, and with shifts of time and place signaled the audience only by the momentary clearing of the stage between the episodes. Information about the identity of the characters and, when necessary, about the time and place of the action was incorporated in the dialogue. No place-headings have been inserted in the present editions; these are apt to obscure the original fluidity of structure, with the emphasis upon action and speech rather than scenic background. (Indications of place are supplied in the footnotes.) The acting, including that of the youthful apprentices to the profession who performed the parts of women, was highly skillful, with a premium placed upon grace of gesture and beauty of diction. The audiences, a cross section of the general public, commonly numbered a thousand, sometimes more than two thousand. Judged by the type of plays they applauded, these audiences were not only large but also perceptive.

THE TEXTS OF THE PLAYS

About half of Shakespeare's plays appeared in print for the first time in the folio volume of 1623. The others had been published individually, usually in quarto volumes, during his lifetime or in the six years following his death. The copy used by the printers of the quartos varied greatly in merit, sometimes representing Shakespeare's true text, sometimes only a debased version of that text. The copy used by the printers of the folio also varied in merit, but was chosen with care. Since it consisted of the best available manuscripts, or the more acceptable quartos (although frequently in editions other than the first), or of quartos corrected by reference to manuscripts, we have good or reasonably good texts of most of the thirty-seven plays.

In the present series, the plays have been newly edited from quarto or folio texts, depending, when a choice offered, upon which is now regarded by bibliographical specialists as the more authoritative. The ideal has been to reproduce the chosen texts with as few alterations as possible, beyond occasional relineation, expansion of abbreviations, and modernization of punctuation and spelling. Emendation is held to a minimum, and such material as has been added, in the way of stage directions and lines supplied by an alternative text, has been enclosed in square brackets.

None of the plays printed in Shakespeare's lifetime were divided into acts and scenes, and the inference is that the author's own manuscripts were not so divided. In the folio collection, some of the plays remained undivided, some were divided into acts, and some were divided into acts and scenes. During the eighteenth century all of the plays were divided into acts and scenes, and in the Cambridge edition of the mid-nineteenth century, from which the influential Globe text derived, this division was more or less regularized and the lines were numbered. Many useful works of reference employ the act–scene–line apparatus thus established.

Since this act–scene division is obviously convenient, but is of very dubious authority so far as Shakespeare's own structural principles are concerned, or the original manner of staging his plays, a problem is presented to modern editors. In the present series the act–scene division is retained marginally, and may be viewed as a reference aid like the line numbering. A star marks the points of division when these points have been determined by a cleared stage indicating a shift of time and place in the action of the play, or when no harm results from the editorial assumption that there is such a shift. However, at those points where the established division is clearly misleading – that is, where continuous action has been split up into separate "scenes" – the star is omitted and the distortion corrected. This mechanical expedient seemed the best means of combining utility and accuracy.

THE GENERAL EDITOR

INTRODUCTION

From the earliest times *The Tragedy of King Richard the Third* has proved one of Shakespeare's most successful plays in the theatre, but the enthusiasms it arouses are of a different order from, let us say, the enthusiasms we feel for a *Macbeth*. It is in fact Shakespeare's most whole-hearted excursion into melodrama, and a brief comparison with a tragedy like *Macbeth*, in certain surface appearances so similar, in so many vital respects so different, can be revealing. Both Richard and Macbeth fascinate us, but our concern for Richard moves only (with the exception of one brief moment in Act V) on the level of admiration for a kind of virtuoso in evil who satisfies us by being so utterly competent, a creation which wins us, partly in spite of ourselves, by his sheer audacity and enormity. Macbeth, however, wins us simply because he is first of all a man, with the glories, failures, and complexities which that proud title carries with it – "What a piece of work is a man!" Of this feeling there is essentially nothing in *Richard III*. Where then lies the secret of the perennial popularity of the play, next to *Hamlet* the most frequently produced of Shakespeare's plays?

In part the answer lies in the uncomplicated, even obvious nature of the play and its principal characters. They wear their hearts upon their sleeves, and no mystery of the unresolved teases an audience into taking thought. An easy virtue perhaps, but one to be reckoned with, especially when it is combined with immense energy, an energy which pervades not only the central character but the play as a whole. From the Marlowe-like opening soliloquy in which Richard with engaging frankness invites us to watch him play the villain to the famous closing cry – "A horse! a horse! my kingdom for a horse!" – Shakespeare rarely allows the pace to slacken or tensions to relax. In one way this effect of pace is achieved through the ruthless handling of historical time, creating always a sense of the pressure both of the moment and of the threatening future. The pattern or formal structure of the play also furthers the effect of pace. As a structural device, Shakespeare, in defiance of history, has introduced the commanding and ominous old Queen Margaret, who, in her choric role (she is nothing but a voice), evokes the past, lashes the present, and forebodes the future, setting up in her memorable curse scene (I, iii) the pattern through which we watch, with a growing sense of the inevitable, the seemingly inexorable march of events. Other devices, similar in effect to the curse pattern – foreshadowing dreams, oaths sworn only to be broken, continual flashes of rather obvious dramatic irony – serve to give form to the play, as, at the same time, they accelerate and regulate its pace. In this connection, Shakespeare's use of the "dramatic moment" deserves particular attention. Little episodes or sudden turns are skillfully exploited to bring out the full theatrical potentiality of the larger and dominating pattern of the scene. For example: the brilliant trick by which Richard turns Margaret's curse upon herself (I, iii); the clever device for announcing Clarence's death (II, i); the strawberry scene heralding the fall of Hastings (III, iv); the clock scene (IV, ii); Richard's abortive attempt to drown out the curses of his mother and Queen Elizabeth with trumpet and drum (IV, iv).

As the center of energy in the play stands Richard himself. Professor E. M. W. Tillyard has well remarked that he is Shakespeare's first character to impress himself upon us as being "larger than life." Shakespeare spares him and us nothing, even heightening the already "monstrous" portrait left for us by his political enemies, and leaving us in no doubt about Richard's ultimate responsibility for all the evil in the play. Such focussing and concentration justifies itself in terms of sheer theatrical effectiveness, and Richard pursues evil with a whole-souled quality which almost achieves a kind of inverted moral significance – he works so hard at being the very best kind of villain. In projecting this character Shakespeare was influenced, of course, by the extreme Elizabethan conception of Machiavellian policy. Already in *3 Henry VI* Richard had promised to "set the murderous Machiavel to school" (III, ii, 193) and had flaunted his rejection of all such human weaknesses as "pity, love, nor fear" – "I am myself alone" (V, vi, 68, 83):

> Why, I can smile, and murder whiles I smile,
> And cry 'Content!' to that which grieves my heart,
> And wet my cheeks with artificial tears,
> And frame my face to all occasions . . . .
> I'll play the orator as well as Nestor,
> Deceive more slily than Ulysses could
> And, like a Sinon, take another Troy.
> I can add colors to the chameleon . . . . (III, ii, 182–91)

Here already is the essential Richard whom Shakespeare presents in the opening lines of *Richard III* : his hypocrisy, his play-acting (cf. *Richard III*, III, v, 1–11), his powers of persuasion, his fox-like slyness (a special attribute of the Machiavellian), above all his virtuosity as a villain. Richard's only virtue is his courage (also granted to him by Shakespeare's sources), though one is tempted to admit his gruesome sense of humor as another. Once only does the audience suffer any real emotional involvement with Richard. When he awakes after the ghostly visitation of his eleven victims, he momentarily exposes himself as a mere man; in place of the brilliant artifact we see a terrified human creature unable to find pity or love in himself even for himself – nothing but fear. It is a moving moment, but to speak of development in Richard's character would be, I think, to set the emphasis in the wrong place and to confuse this play with Shakespearean tragedy. Richard is a static character; he emerges complete at the very beginning and never undergoes any basic change. "I am determinèd to prove a villain," he says, and the play consists largely in our watching breathlessly as he moves from crime to crime keeping his promise to us. Such singleness and simplicity of purpose has, of course, both structural and dramatic value, but we never really allow ourselves to be blinded to the limitations which, like other aspects of this play, it imposes ultimately on the kind of play Shakespeare is writing.

The Tragedy of King Richard the Third, or, as it is perhaps better described in the running titles of the first folio, The Life and Death of Richard the Third, may safely be dated between 1591 and 1594. For historical materials Shakespeare turned, as in his other English history plays, to the second edition of Holinshed's Chronicles (1587), a compilation drawing heavily, through Hall's Chronicle (1550), on the celebrated Life of Richard the Third usually attributed to Sir Thomas More and on Polydore Vergil's Historia Anglica (1534). A few details may be traced directly to Hall. Both More's Life (if indeed More and not Cardinal Morton was the author) and Polydore Vergil's account are savagely anti-Yorkist, and the portrait of Richard which emerges is darkly colored and almost wholly unfavorable. Curiously different is the verdict of many modern historians who tend to equal extremes in rehabilitating Richard. For the average reader, however, Shakespeare has once and for all settled Richard's character – as well try, in the words of a favorite Elizabethan proverb, to wash the Ethiop! In addition to his use of the chronicles, Shakespeare probably owes a few suggestions to an anonymous play, The True Tragedie of Richard the

Third (printed 1594), and possibly even to the early three-part Latin play *Richardus Tertius* (1579) by Thomas Legge.

An extreme, but not uncharacteristic, example of Shakespeare's dramatic treatment of history may be found in the two opening scenes. In the first, Shakespeare combines events of 1477 (the arrest of Clarence), of 1483 (the reported final sickness of Edward IV), and of 1471 (the projected marriage of Richard with Lady Anne), the last date being underscored by Richard's opening soliloquy which implies the beginning of Edward's reign. This preparation leads directly into the second scene: the funeral procession of the recently dead Henry VI (1471), a situation which is made to serve for the occasion of Richard's triumphantly outrageous wooing of Lady Anne, daughter-in-law of Henry VI and widow of his son, Edward, Prince of Wales, both his victims. Thus with a few bold strokes Shakespeare highhandedly telescopes and confuses the events of thirteen years, reducing them, as it were, to a single moment. With what justification, we may ask. The answer: art and the theatre. With Richard as the center of his play, Shakespeare is most vitally concerned to concentrate on him any situation which can be made to exploit the immediate dramatic potentialities of his character; for this he needs the Clarence affair and the Anne wooing, both nicely calculated to play up different facets of Richard's personality. For the same reason, Edward IV must be relegated to a subordinate role and dismissed from the play with a quick hand. Even as he recognizes all this and arranges for it, Shakespeare also senses the dramatic advantage of preserving an immediate continuity with *3 Henry VI* by picking up the story where that play had left it – with Richard's murder of Henry VI and the accession of Edward IV. In the place of history, time, and logic Shakespeare gives us a dramatic fiction, a play.

Paradoxically, however, *Richard III* remains very much a "history" play, for Shakespeare is here deeply concerned with political themes: the role of the king, good (Henry) and bad (Richard), with an intermediate type in Edward IV; Richard both as the type of the Scourge of God, working out England's crime in the deposition and murder of Richard II, and as the "unsuccessive" tyrant whom, even under Tudor doctrine, it was righteous to depose; the emergence of the great Tudor dynasty under the newly crowned Lancastrian Henry VII, who by his marriage to the Yorkist Princess Elizabeth was to heal the long-festering wounds of the Wars of the Roses. One must always remember, too, that *Richard III* is the last in a series of eight closely interrelated plays (though at this time only the three parts of *Henry VI* had been written) and that throughout it Shakespeare is careful by reference and allusion (particularly through the figure of old Queen Margaret) to preserve a sense of a larger historical continuity – of the flow of events seen in terms of cause and effect, of a past and a future, as well as of a bare present.

In style and diction *Richard III* belongs markedly to Shakespeare's early serious manner, a manner much influenced by the University playwrights, Marlowe and Greene, sometimes to such a degree that it is difficult to recognize Shakespeare's special idiom. In general the style is more rhetorical than poetic, depending for its effect upon a variety of artificial and cleverly manipulated figures or "flowers of rhetoric." In many ways, of course, it is the perfect instrument for a Richard – witty, hard, and brilliantly efficient, always glancing, parrying, thrusting. This effect comes out most obviously in the rapier-like exchanges (a development of Senecan stichomythia, one of a great many Senecan traces in the play) between Richard and Lady Anne (I, ii) or Richard and Queen Elizabeth (IV, iv). Like so many of the other rhetorical devices in the play, this device depends for its effect on some variety of verbal or structural "repetition": of words within the line to give a turn of thought or play on words, of words or phrases linking line to line, of phrase balanced against phrase, of line against line, of speech against speech. But it must be noticed that although this wrought and over-wrought kind of verse sets the dominant stylistic tone and is admirably effective in realizing for us the peculiarly hard-edged, amoral world on the surface of which the characters move, it does not exclude a great deal of stylistic variety even within itself. Moreover, in contrast are the moments of sudden racy colloquialism – like a breath of fresh air – most of which occur in Richard's speeches and lend him a personal turn of speech which we quickly come to recognize as peculiarly a part of him. In this respect, as critics have noticed, he is Shakespeare's first character to possess a "voice" of his own. To this may be added some occasional touches of effective pathos in lines like those at IV, i, 97–103 and the grimly humorous prose of the First and Second Murderers, an early example of Shakespeare's use of comedy to intensify the horror of the moment, here set against a background of what are almost the only imaginatively poetic speeches in the whole play – those in which Clarence relates his dream (I, iv). These and some later speeches of Clarence in the same scene look forward to the kind of poetry with which, a year or two later, Shakespeare endows Richard II and which, in its turn, becomes the perfect medium for expressing the weak, indeterminate, word-drunk king – one, so unlike Richard III, with no capacity for a "world . . . to bustle in."

The Restoration and earlier eighteenth century were temperamentally given to "improving" Shakespeare's plays, and in 1700 Colley Cibber produced his version of *Richard III*. Briefly, Cibber omits Edward IV, Clarence, and Queen Margaret and begins the play just before Richard's murder of Henry VI. The result is a generally tightened-up play which is even more theatrical than Shakespeare's. For roughly a hundred and fifty years Cibber's version, with slight changes, held the stage un-challenged, and Cibber's lines "Off with his head – so much for Buckingham!" and "Conscience avaunt!

Richard's himself again!" are often understandably attributed to Shakespeare. Even today Cibber is still very much alive. Witness Sir Lawrence Olivier's motion picture version which drew heavily not only on Cibber but on Cibber's "improver," David Garrick! There is perhaps a moral worth pondering here, for Cibber's longevity is unique among the many "improvers" of Shakespearean plays, and *Richard III* is the only Shakespearean play in which we can still tolerate an alien hand.

Harvard University   G. BLAKEMORE EVANS

NOTE ON THE TEXT

Richard III was first printed in quarto form in 1597 from copy evidently representing the communal effort of the acting company to reconstruct the play when deprived of their regular prompt-book. There were seven additional quarto editions, Quarto 6 (1622), after correction against an independent manuscript, presumably serving as copy for the first folio text (1623), except for two sections (III, i, 1–158, and V, iii, 48 to end) which appear to have been set up from an uncorrected copy of Quarto 3 (1602). The textual problem involved is one of the most complex in Shakespeare, and is further discussed in the appendix. The present edition is based on the folio text, with the addition, in square brackets, of about thirty-three lines from the first quarto, the most important group being IV, ii, 97–115. The quartos are undivided into acts and scenes. The folio text is divided, and this division received editorial elaboration: III, iv became III, iv, v, vi, vii; IV, ii became IV, ii, iii; and V, ii became V, ii, iii, iv, v. In the present edition the editorial divisions are indicated marginally, but those scenes improperly split by early editors are printed continuously, and stars are placed only at those points where there is actually a vacated stage signalling a change in time, place, or both. Stage directions not in the folio are bracketed even though they may appear in the quartos.

THE TRAGEDY OF
KING RICHARD
THE THIRD

King Edward the Fourth

Edward, Prince of Wales, afterwards Edward V } sons to
Richard, Duke of York } the King

George, Duke of Clarence } brothers
Richard, Duke of Gloucester, afterwards } to the
    Richard III } King

A young Son of Clarence (Edward Plantagenet,
    Earl of Warwick)
Henry, Earl of Richmond, afterwards Henry VII
Cardinal Bourchier, Archbishop of Canterbury
Thomas Rotherham, Archbishop of York
John Morton, Bishop of Ely
Duke of Buckingham
Duke of Norfolk
Earl of Surrey, his son
Anthony Woodeville, Earl Rivers, brother to Queen
    Elizabeth
Marquess of Dorset and Lord Grey, her sons
Earl of Oxford
Lord Hastings
Lord Stanley (also called Earl of Derby)
Lord Lovel
Sir Thomas Vaughan
Sir Richard Ratcliffe
Sir William Catesby
Sir James Tyrrel
Sir James Blunt
Sir Walter Herbert
Sir Robert Brakenbury, Lieutenant of the Tower
Keeper in the Tower
Sir William Brandon
Christopher Urswick, a priest
Lord Mayor of London
Sheriff of Wiltshire
Tressel and Berkeley, gentlemen attending on Lady Anne

24

Ghosts of Henry VI ; Edward, Prince of Wales, his son ; and
   other victims of Richard
Elizabeth, Queen to Edward IV
Margaret, widow of Henry VI
Duchess of York, mother to Edward IV, Gloucester, and
   Clarence
Lady Anne, widow of Edward, Prince of Wales, son to
   Henry VI ; afterwards married to Richard, Duke of
   Gloucester
A young Daughter of Clarence (Lady Margaret
   Plantagenet)
Lords, Gentlemen, and other Attendants ; a Pursuivant
   (Hastings), a Page, a Scrivener, a Priest, Bishops,
   Citizens, Aldermen, Councillors, Murderers,
   Messengers, Soldiers, &c.

   Scene : London and other parts of England]

Lancaster is York

Henry VI   Ed IV

THE TRAGEDY OF
KING RICHARD
THE THIRD

Enter Richard, Duke of Gloucester, solus. [handwritten: soliloquy]   I, i

RICHARD

Now is the winter of our discontent   [handwritten: refers to battle]
Made glorious summer by this son of York;   2
And all the clouds that lowered upon our house
In the deep bosom of the ocean buried.
Now are our brows bound with victorious wreaths,
Our bruisèd arms hung up for monuments,   6
Our stern alarums changed to merry meetings,   7
Our dreadful marches to delightful measures.   8
Grim-visaged war hath smoothed his wrinklèd front,   9
And now, instead of mounting barbèd steeds   10
To fright the souls of fearful adversaries,   [handwritten: war: horrible]
He capers nimbly in a lady's chamber   [handwritten: hideous appearance vs]
To the lascivious pleasing of a lute.   [handwritten: trying to be seductive]   13
But I, that am not shaped for sportive tricks
Nor made to court an amorous looking-glass;
I, that am rudely stamped, and want love's majesty
To strut before a wanton ambling nymph;   [handwritten: killing figure]
I, that am curtailed of this fair proportion,
Cheated of feature by dissembling Nature,   19

I, i A London street   **2** *son* (with play on 'sun')   **6** *arms* armor; *monuments* memorials   **7** *alarums* calls to arms   **8** *measures* stately dances   **9** *front* forehead   **10** *barbèd* armed with protective covering, studded or spiked, on breast and flanks   **11** *fearful* timid   **13** *lascivious pleasing* seductive charm   **17** *ambling* walking affectedly   **19** *feature* form of body; *dissembling* deceiving (because my greatness is cloaked by a false appearance)

27

Deformed, unfinished, sent before my time
21 Into this breathing world, scarce half made up,
22 And that so lamely and unfashionable
That dogs bark at me as I halt by them –
24 Why I, in this weak piping time of peace,
Have no delight to pass away the time,
Unless to see my shadow in the sun
27 And descant on mine own deformity.
And therefore, since I cannot prove a lover
To entertain these fair well-spoken days,
I am determinèd to prove a villain
And hate the idle pleasures of these days.
32 Plots have I laid, inductions dangerous,
33 By drunken prophecies, libels, and dreams,
To set my brother Clarence and the king
In deadly hate the one against the other;
And if King Edward be as true and just
As I am subtle, false, and treacherous,
38 This day should Clarence closely be mewed up
About a prophecy which says that G
Of Edward's heirs the murderer shall be.
Dive, thoughts, down to my soul – here Clarence comes!

Enter Clarence guarded, and Brakenbury
[Lieutenant of the Tower].

Brother, good day. What means this armèd guard
That waits upon your grace?
CLARENCE   His majesty,
44 Tend'ring my person's safety, hath appointed
45 This conduct to convey me to the Tower.

---

21 *breathing* living   22 *unfashionable* misshapen (cf. I, ii, 250)   24 *piping* (the pipe or recorder was associated with peace, as the fife with war)   27 *descant* compose variations on a simple theme (the speech illustrates this line: the theme, Richard's deformity)   32 *inductions* initial plans   33 *drunken prophecies* prophecies uttered under the influence of drink   38 *mewed up* imprisoned (cf. l. 132)   44 *Tend'ring* being concerned for (irony)   45 *conduct* escort; *convey* conduct (with play on 'steal'); *Tower* the Tower of London (frequently used as a prison)

RICHARD
Upon what cause?

CLARENCE   Because my name is George.

RICHARD
Alack, my lord, that fault is none of yours:
He should for that commit your godfathers.
O, belike his majesty hath some intent   49
That you should be new christ'ned in the Tower.   50
But what's the matter, Clarence, may I know?

CLARENCE
Yea, Richard, when I know; for I protest
As yet I do not. But, as I can learn,
He hearkens after prophecies and dreams,
And from the cross-row plucks the letter G,   55
And says a wizard told him that by G   56
His issue disinherited should be.
And, for my name of George begins with G,
It follows in his thought that I am he.
These (as I learn) and suchlike toys as these   60
Hath moved his highness to commit me now.

RICHARD
Why this it is, when men are ruled by women:
'Tis not the king that sends you to the Tower;
My Lady Grey his wife, Clarence, 'tis she
That tempers him to this extremity.   65
Was it not she, and that good man of worship,
Anthony Woodeville, her brother there,   67
That made him send Lord Hastings to the Tower,
From whence this present day he is deliverèd?
We are not safe, Clarence – we are not safe.

CLARENCE
By heaven, I think there is no man is secure

49 *belike* probably   50 *new christ'ned* (anticipates, ironically, Clarence's drowning in I, iv)   55 *cross-row* alphabet   56 *wizard* wise man or male witch   60 *toys* trifles, fancies   65 *tempers* moulds   67 *Woodeville* i.e. Earl Rivers (trisyllabic)

72   But the queen's kindred, and night-walking heralds
73   That trudge betwixt the king and Mistress Shore.
      Heard you not what an humble suppliant
      Lord Hastings was for his delivery?

RICHARD

      Humbly complaining to her deity
      Got my Lord Chamberlain his liberty.
      I'll tell you what, I think it is our way,
      If we will keep in favor with the king,
      To be her men and wear her livery.
81   The jealous o'erworn widow and herself,
82   Since that our brother dubbed them gentlewomen,
83   Are mighty gossips in our monarchy.

BRAKENBURY

      I beseech your graces both to pardon me:
85   His majesty hath straitly given in charge
      That no man shall have private conference
      (Of what degree soever) with your brother.

RICHARD

88   Even so? An please your worship, Brakenbury,
      You may partake of anything we say.
      We speak no treason, man. We say the king
      Is wise and virtuous, and his noble queen
92   Well struck in years, fair, and not jealous.
      We say that Shore's wife hath a pretty foot,
      A cherry lip, a bonny eye, a passing pleasing tongue;
      And that the queen's kindred are made gentlefolks.
      How say you, sir? Can you deny all this?

BRAKENBURY

97   With this, my lord, myself have nought to do.

72 *night-walking heralds* i.e. secret messengers (agents of assignation)   73
Mistress Shore i.e. Jane Shore, mistress of Edward IV ('mistress,' however,
was regularly applied to any woman, married or unmarried, as a title of respect)   81 *widow* i.e. Queen Elizabeth (cf. l. 109)   82 *dubbed* knighted (a
malicious pairing of Queen Elizabeth and Mistress Shore entirely without
basis)   83 *gossips* (people, traditionally, with a lot to say)   85 *straitly* strictly
88 *An* if   92 *Well struck in years* (a politic way of saying 'old')   97 *nought*
nothing

[handwritten: R playing his act pretending to be very respectable for putting Clarence in jail.]

RICHARD

Naught to do with Mistress Shore? I tell thee, fellow,
He that doth naught with her (excepting one)   99
Were best to do it secretly alone.

BRAKENBURY

What one, my lord?

RICHARD

Her husband, knave. Wouldst thou betray me?

BRAKENBURY

I do beseech your grace to pardon me, and withal   103
Forbear your conference with the noble duke.

CLARENCE

We know thy charge, Brakenbury, and will obey.

RICHARD

We are the queen's abjects, and must obey.   106
Brother, farewell. I will unto the king;
And whatsoe'er you will employ me in,
Were it to call King Edward's widow sister,
I will perform it to enfranchise you.   110
Meantime, this deep disgrace in brotherhood.   111
Touches me deeper than you can imagine.

CLARENCE

I know it pleaseth neither of us well.

RICHARD

Well, your imprisonment shall not be long:
I will deliver you, or else lie for you.   115
Meantime, have patience.

CLARENCE   I must perforce. Farewell.   116
              Exit Clarence [with Brakenbury and Guard].

RICHARD

Go, tread the path that thou shalt ne'er return:
Simple plain Clarence, I do love thee so

[handwritten: what a fool, I'm going to put you out of your misery]

99 *naught* i.e. the sexual act   103 *withal* at the same time   106 *abjects*
most servile subjects (with play on 'outcasts')   110 *enfranchise* release
from confinement   111-12 *disgrace . . . imagine* (with an obvious double
meaning)   115 *lie for* go to prison in place of (with play on 'tell lies about')
116 *perforce* of necessity

That I will shortly send thy soul to heaven,
If heaven will take the present at our hands.
But who comes here? The new-deliverèd Hastings?
          Enter Lord Hastings.

HASTINGS
Good time of day unto my gracious lord.

RICHARD
As much unto my good Lord Chamberlain.
Well are you welcome to the open air.
125   How hath your lordship brooked imprisonment?

HASTINGS
With patience, noble lord, as prisoners must;
But I shall live, my lord, to give them thanks
That were the cause of my imprisonment.

RICHARD
No doubt, no doubt; and so shall Clarence too,
For they that were your enemies are his
And have prevailed as much on him as you.

HASTINGS
More pity that the eagles should be mewed,
Whiles kites and buzzards prey at liberty.

RICHARD
What news abroad?

HASTINGS
No news so bad abroad as this at home:
The king is sickly, weak, and melancholy,
And his physicians fear him mightily.

RICHARD
Now, by Saint John, that news is bad indeed!
O, he hath kept an evil diet long
140   And overmuch consumed his royal person:
'Tis very grievous to be thought upon.
Where is he? In his bed?

HASTINGS He is.

125 *brooked* tolerated

32

[handwritten: R—vengeful, bitter, angry, hateful]
[handwritten: good at being bad ← deception in speech]

[handwritten: Shakesp. doesn't want us to sympatheze w/ R.]

RICHARD

Go you before, and I will follow you.   *Exit Hastings.*
He cannot live, I hope, and must not die
Till George be packed with posthorse up to heaven.   146
I'll in, to urge his hatred more to Clarence   147
With lies well steeled with weighty arguments;   148
And, if I fail not in my deep intent,
Clarence hath not another day to live:
Which done, God take King Edward to his mercy *[handwritten: world is his toy]*
And leave the world for me to bustle in! → *[handwritten: world toy]*
For then I'll marry Warwick's youngest daughter.   153
What though I killed her husband and her father?
The readiest way to make the wench amends
→ Is to become her husband and her father:
The which will I – not all so much for love
As for another secret close intent   158
By marrying her which I must reach unto.
But yet I run before my horse to market:
→ Clarence still breathes; Edward still lives and reigns;
→ When they are gone, then must I count my gains.   *Exit.*

[right margin handwritten: Clarence has to die first]

*

Enter the corse of Henry the Sixth, with Halberds to   I, ii
guard it; Lady Anne being the mourner [attended
by Tressel and Berkeley].

ANNE

Set down, set down your honorable load –
If honor may be shrouded in a hearse –
Whilst I awhile obsequiously lament   3

---

146 *with posthorse* (figuratively, the quickest way)   147 *urge ... to* incite his
anger more against   148 *steeled* strengthened as with iron   153 *Warwick's
youngest daughter* i.e. Lady Anne, widow of Prince Edward   158 *secret close
intent* (Richard, aiming at the throne, schemes to ally himself with the line of
Lancaster as a useful preliminary move)
I, ii The same   s.d. *corse* corpse; *Halberds* halberdiers (guards, carrying
halberds; see l. 40 below)   3 *obsequiously* in a manner fitting a funeral

Th' untimely fall of virtuous Lancaster.
[The Bearers set down the hearse.]
5 Poor key-cold figure of a holy king,
Pale ashes of the house of Lancaster,
Thou bloodless remnant of that royal blood,
Be it lawful that I invocate thy ghost
To hear the lamentations of poor Anne,
Wife to thy Edward, to thy slaught'red son
Stabbed by the selfsame hand that made these wounds!
Lo, in these windows that let forth thy life
13 I pour the helpless balm of my poor eyes.
O, cursèd be the hand that made these holes!
Cursèd the heart that had the heart to do it!
Cursèd the blood that let this blood from hence!
17 More direful hap betide that hated wretch
That makes us wretched by the death of thee
Than I can wish to wolves – to spiders, toads,
Or any creeping venomed thing that lives!
If ever he have child, abortive be it,
22 Prodigious, and untimely brought to light,
Whose ugly and unnatural aspect
May fright the hopeful mother at the view,
25 And that be heir to his unhappiness!
If ever he have wife, let her be made
More miserable by the life of him
Than I am made by my young lord and thee!
29 Come, now towards Chertsey with your holy load,
30 Taken from Paul's to be interrèd there.
[The Bearers take up the hearse.]
31 And still, as you are weary of this weight,
32 Rest you, whiles I lament King Henry's corse.

---

5 *key-cold* very cold (as a metal key)   13 *helpless* affording no help   17 *hap betide* fortune befall   22 *Prodigious* unnatural, monstrous   25 *unhappiness* innate evil   29 *Chertsey* the monastery of Chertsey near London   30 *Paul's* St Paul's Cathedral, London   31 *still, as* whenever   32 *whiles I lament* during which time I will lament

34

Enter Richard, Duke of Gloucester.

RICHARD
  Stay, you that bear the corse, and set it down.

ANNE
  What black magician conjures up this fiend
  To stop devoted charitable deeds?   35

RICHARD
  Villains, set down the corse, or, by Saint Paul,
  I'll make a corse of him that disobeys!

GENTLEMAN
  My lord, stand back, and let the coffin pass.

RICHARD
  Unmannered dog! Stand thou, when I command!   39
  Advance thy halberd higher than my breast,   40
  Or, by Saint Paul, I'll strike thee to my foot
  And spurn upon thee, beggar, for thy boldness.   42
  [The Bearers set down the hearse.]

ANNE
  What, do you tremble? Are you all afraid?
  Alas, I blame you not, for you are mortal,
  And mortal eyes cannot endure the devil.
  Avaunt, thou dreadful minister of hell!
  Thou hadst but power over his mortal body;
  His soul thou canst not have. Therefore, be gone.

RICHARD
  Sweet saint, for charity, be not so curst.   49

ANNE
  Foul devil, for God's sake hence, and trouble us not,
  For thou hast made the happy earth thy hell,   51
  Filled it with cursing cries and deep exclaims.
  If thou delight to view thy heinous deeds,
  Behold this pattern of thy butcheries.   54
  O gentlemen, see! See dead Henry's wounds

---

35 *devoted* sacred   39 *Stand* halt   40 *Advance . . . breast* raise your halberd
(a long-handled poleaxe with a pike attached) to upright position   42 *spurn
upon* stamp under foot   49 *curst* shrewish   51 *happy* naturally pleasant
54 *pattern* example

56 Open their congealed mouths and bleed afresh!
    Blush, blush, thou lump of foul deformity;
58 For 'tis thy presence that exhales this blood
    From cold and empty veins where no blood dwells.
    Thy deeds inhuman and unnatural
    Provokes this deluge most unnatural.
    O God, which this blood mad'st, revenge his death!
    O earth, which this blood drink'st, revenge his death!
    Either heav'n with lightning strike the murd'rer dead;
65 Or earth gape open wide and eat him quick,
    As thou dost swallow up this good king's blood
    Which his hell-governed arm hath butcherèd!

RICHARD
    Lady, you know no rules of charity,
    Which renders good for bad, blessings for curses.

ANNE
    Villain, thou know'st nor law of God nor man:
    No beast so fierce but knows some touch of pity.

RICHARD
    But I know none, and therefore am no beast.

ANNE
    O wonderful, when devils tell the truth!

RICHARD
    More wonderful, when angels are so angry.
    Vouchsafe, divine perfection of a woman,
    Of these supposèd crimes to give me leave
    By circumstance but to acquit myself.

ANNE
78 Vouchsafe, diffused infection of a man,
    Of these known evils, but to give me leave
    By circumstance t' accuse thy cursèd self.

RICHARD
    Fairer than tongue can name thee, let me have
    Some patient leisure to excuse myself.

---

56 *bleed afresh* (in popular belief the wounds of a murdered man bled in the presence of the murderer)   58 *exhales* draws out   65 *quick* alive   78 *diffused infection* shapeless plague (more for sound than sense; cf. l. 75)

ANNE

 Fouler than heart can think thee, thou canst make
 No excuse current but to hang thyself.   84

RICHARD

 By such despair I should accuse myself.

ANNE

 And by despairing shalt thou stand excusèd
 For doing worthy vengeance on thyself
 That didst unworthy slaughter upon others.

RICHARD

 Say that I slew them not?

ANNE   Then say they were not slain.
 But dead they are, and, devilish slave, by thee.

RICHARD

 I did not kill your husband.

ANNE   Why, then he is alive.

RICHARD

 Nay, he is dead, and slain by Edward's hands.

ANNE

 In thy foul throat thou li'st! Queen Margaret saw
 Thy murd'rous falchion smoking in his blood;   94
 The which thou once didst bend against her breast,
 But that thy brothers beat aside the point.

RICHARD

 I was provokèd by her sland'rous tongue
 That laid their guilt upon my guiltless shoulders.

ANNE

 Thou wast provokèd by thy bloody mind
 That never dream'st on aught but butcheries.
 Didst thou not kill this king?

RICHARD   I grant ye.

ANNE

 Dost grant me, hedgehog? Then God grant me too
 Thou mayst be damnèd for that wicked deed!
 O, he was gentle, mild, and virtuous!

---

84 *current* authentic or acceptable 94 *falchion* slightly hooked sword

Richard killed 37
Henry VI

he loves the verbal seduction

is better for God that this in heaven

RICHARD
The better for the King of Heaven that hath him.

ANNE
He is in heaven, where thou shalt never come.

RICHARD
107   Let him thank me that holp to send him thither;
For he was fitter for that place than earth.

ANNE
And thou unfit for any place, but hell.

RICHARD
Yes, one place else, if you will hear me name it.

ANNE
Some dungeon.

RICHARD   Your bedchamber.

ANNE
Ill rest betide the chamber where thou liest!

RICHARD
So will it, madam, till I lie with you.

ANNE
I hope so.

RICHARD   I know so. But, gentle Lady Anne,
To leave this keen encounter of our wits
And fall something into a slower method –
117   Is not the causer of the timeless deaths
Of these Plantagenets, Henry and Edward,
As blameful as the executioner?

ANNE
120   Thou wast the cause and most accursed effect.

RICHARD
Your beauty was the cause of that effect –
Your beauty, that did haunt me in my sleep
To undertake the death of all the world,
So I might live one hour in your sweet bosom.

*she becomes the performer,
he becomes the director*

107 *holp* helped   117 *timeless* untimely   120 *effect* i.e. executioner (l. 119)
or efficient agent

*hearse
bearers – a
new audience*

38

*Anne – has to
get the last
word*

he flatters her
he did it because
she is beautiful—
She gets quite
rowdy—is not
purely victim.

ANNE
　If I thought that, I tell thee, <u>homicide</u>,
　These nails should rent that beauty from my cheeks. 125

RICHARD
　These eyes could not endure that beauty's <u>wrack</u>; 127
　You should not blemish it, if I stood by:
　As all the world is cheerèd by the sun,
　So I by that. It is my day, my life.

she loses her
hatred to
him.

ANNE
　Black night o'ershade thy day, and death thy life!

RICHARD
　Curse not thyself, fair creature – thou art both.

ANNE
　I would I were, to be revenged on thee.

RICHARD
　It is a quarrel most unnatural,
　To be revenged on him that loveth thee.

ANNE
　It is a quarrel just and reasonable,
　To be revenged on him that killed my husband.

RICHARD
　He that bereft thee, lady, of thy husband,
　Did it to help thee to a better husband.

ANNE
　His better doth not breathe upon the earth. 140

RICHARD
　He lives, that loves thee better than he could.

ANNE
　Name him.

RICHARD　　　Plantagenet.

ANNE　　　　　　　　Why that was he.

RICHARD
　The selfsame name, but one of better nature.

ANNE
　Where is he?

125 *homicide* murderer　127 *wrack* ruin

Richard wants to
marry Anne

RICHARD   Here.
　　　　[She] spits at him. Why dost thou spit at me?
ANNE
　　Would it were mortal poison for thy sake!
RICHARD
　　Never came poison from so sweet a place.
ANNE
147　Never hung poison on a fouler toad.
　　Out of my sight! Thou dost infect mine eyes.
RICHARD
149　Thine eyes, sweet lady, have infected mine.
ANNE
150　Would they were basilisks to strike thee dead!
RICHARD
151　I would they were, that I might die at once;
　　For now they kill me with a living death.
　　Those eyes of thine from mine have drawn salt tears,
154　Shamed their aspects with store of childish drops:
　　These eyes, which never shed remorseful tear –
　　No, when my father York and Edward wept
　　To hear the piteous moan that Rutland made
158　When black-faced Clifford shook his sword at him;
159　Nor when thy warlike father, like a child,
　　Told the sad story of my father's death
　　And twenty times made pause to sob and weep,
　　That all the standers-by had wet their cheeks
　　Like trees bedashed with rain – in that sad time
　　My manly eyes did scorn an humble tear;
　　And what these sorrows could not thence exhale,
　　Thy beauty hath, and made them blind with weeping.
　　I never sued to friend nor enemy;

147 *poison . . . toad* (toads were considered venomous)   149 *eyes . . . mine*
(the eyes were believed to be the entry-ports of love)   150 *basilisks* fabulous
reptiles capable of killing with a look   151 *at once* once and for all   154
aspects glances   158 *black-faced* gloomy, evilly portentous   159 *thy . . .
father* i.e. Richard Nevil, Earl of Warwick, known as the 'King-maker'

My tongue could never learn sweet smoothing word ;   168
But, now thy beauty is proposed my fee,
My proud heart sues, and prompts my tongue to speak.
    She looks scornfully at him.
Teach not thy lip such scorn ; for it was made
For kissing, lady, not for such contempt.
If thy revengeful heart cannot forgive,
Lo, here I lend thee this sharp-pointed sword,
Which if thou please to hide in this true breast
And let the soul forth that adoreth thee,
I lay it naked to the deadly stroke   177
And humbly beg the death upon my knee.
    *He lays his breast open. She offers at [it] with his
    sword.*
Nay, do not pause : for I did kill King Henry –
But 'twas thy beauty that provokèd me.
Nay, now dispatch : 'twas I that stabbed young Edward –
But 'twas thy heavenly face that set me on.   182
    She falls the sword.
Take up the sword again, or take up me.

ANNE
    Arise, dissembler : though I wish thy death,
    I will not be thy executioner.

RICHARD
    Then bid me kill myself, and I will do it.

ANNE
    I have already.

RICHARD   That was in thy rage :
    Speak it again, and even with the word
    This hand, which for thy love did kill thy love,
    Shall for thy love kill a far truer love ;
    To both their deaths shalt thou be accessary.   191

ANNE
    I would I knew thy heart.

---

168 *smoothing* flattering   177 *naked* (1) bare, (2) unarmed   182 s.d. *falls*
drops   191 *accessary* acceding

41

RICHARD
　'Tis figured in my tongue.

ANNE
　I fear me both are false.

RICHARD
　Then never was man true.

ANNE
　Well, well, put up your sword.

RICHARD
　Say then my peace is made.

ANNE
　That shalt thou know hereafter.

RICHARD
　But shall I live in hope?

ANNE
　All men, I hope, live so.

[RICHARD]
　Vouchsafe to wear this ring.

[ANNE
　To take is not to give.]
　　　　[*Richard slips the ring on her finger.*]

RICHARD
　Look how my ring encompasseth thy finger,
　Even so thy breast encloseth my poor heart:
　Wear both of them, for both of them are thine.
206　And if thy poor devoted servant may
　But beg one favor at thy gracious hand,
　Thou dost confirm his happiness for ever.

ANNE What is it?

RICHARD
　That it may please you leave these sad designs
　To him that hath most cause to be a mourner,
212　And presently repair to Crosby House;
　Where – after I have solemnly interred

206 *servant* (1) one in subjection, (2) lover　212 *presently* at once; *Crosby House* (Richard's center of operations)

At Chertsey monast'ry this noble king
And wet his grave with my repentant tears –
I will with all expedient duty see you.   216
For divers unknown reasons I beseech you,   217
Grant me this boon.

ANNE
With all my heart ; and much it joys me too
To see you are become so penitent.
Tressel and Berkeley, go along with me.

RICHARD
Bid me farewell.

ANNE   'Tis more than you deserve ;   222
But since you teach me how to flatter you,
Imagine I have said farewell already.
                    Exeunt two [Tressel and Berkeley], with Anne.

[RICHARD
Sirs, take up the corse.]

GENTLEMAN   Towards Chertsey, noble lord ?

RICHARD
No, to Whitefriars – there attend my coming.   226
                    Exit [Guard with Bearers and] corse.
Was ever woman in this humor wooed ?
Was ever woman in this humor won ?
I'll have her, but I will not keep her long.
What ? I that killed her husband and his father
To take her in her heart's extremest hate,
With curses in her mouth, tears in her eyes,
The bleeding witness of my hatred by,
Having God, her conscience, and these bars against me,
And I no friends to back my suit at all
But the plain devil and dissembling looks ?
And yet to win her ! All the world to nothing !   237
Ha !

he doesn't respect the "good world" is pathetic

---

216 *expedient* speedy   217 *unknown* secret   222 *'Tis . . . deserve* i.e. to fare
well is more than you deserve   226 *Whitefriars* a Carmelite priory, south of
Fleet Street, London   237 *All . . . nothing* all odds against me

Hath she forgot already that brave prince,
Edward, her lord, whom I, some three months since,
241   Stabbed in my angry mood at Tewkesbury?
A sweeter and a lovelier gentleman,
243   Framed in the prodigality of nature –
Young, valiant, wise, and (no doubt) right royal –
The spacious world cannot again afford;
246   And will she yet abase her eyes on me,
247   That cropped the golden prime of this sweet prince
And made her widow to a woeful bed?
249   On me, whose all not equals Edward's moi'ty?
On me, that halts and am misshapen thus?
251   My dukedom to a beggarly denier,
I do mistake my person all this while!
Upon my life, she finds (although I cannot)
254   Myself to be a marv'llous proper man.
255   I'll be at charges for a looking-glass
And entertain a score or two of tailors
To study fashions to adorn my body:
Since I am crept in favor with myself,
I will maintain it with some little cost.
260   But first I'll turn yon fellow in his grave,
And then return lamenting to my love.
Shine out, fair sun, till I have bought a glass,
That I may see my shadow as I pass.   *Exit.*

*[handwritten margin notes: she loves him / she loves because she's / too strong, but not strong enough *]*

241 *Tewkesbury* (scene of the battle in which the Lancastrians were finally defeated and Prince Edward killed) 243 *prodigality* profuseness 246 *abase* cast down or make base 247 *cropped . . . prince* i.e. cut him off in the flower of youth 249 *moi'ty* half 251 *denier* copper coin, twelfth of a sou (dissyllabic) 254 *marv'llous proper* wonderfully handsome 255 *at charges for* at the expense of 260 *in* into

Enter the Queen Mother [Elizabeth], Lord Rivers,   I, iii
[Marquess of Dorset,] and Lord Grey.

RIVERS
Have patience, madam; there's no doubt his majesty
→Will soon recover his accustomed health.

GREY
In that you brook it ill, it makes him worse: 3
Therefore for God's sake entertain good comfort
And cheer his grace with quick and merry eyes.

QUEEN ELIZABETH
If he were dead, what would betide on me?   6

GREY
No other harm but loss of such a lord.

QUEEN ELIZABETH
The loss of such a lord includes all harms.

GREY
→ The heavens have blessed you with a goodly son
To be your comforter when he is gone.

QUEEN ELIZABETH
Ah, he is young; and his minority
→ Is put unto the trust of Richard Gloucester,
A man that loves not me, nor none of you.

RIVERS
Is it concluded he shall be Protector?

QUEEN ELIZABETH
It is determined, not concluded yet: 15
But so it must be, if the king miscarry.
        Enter Buckingham and [Stanley, Earl of] Derby.

GREY
Here come the lords of Buckingham and Derby.

BUCKINGHAM
Good time of day unto your royal grace!

DERBY
God make your majesty joyful, as you have been!

I, iii The royal palace   3 *brook* endure   6 *betide on* happen to   15 *determined, not concluded* resolved, not officially decreed

QUEEN ELIZABETH

20   The Countess Richmond, good my Lord of Derby,
      To your good prayer will scarcely say 'Amen.'
      Yet, Derby, notwithstanding she's your wife
  →   And loves not me, be you, good lord, assured
      I hate not you for her proud arrogance.

DERBY

      I do beseech you, either not believe
      The envious slanders of her false accusers;
      Or, if she be accused on true report,
      Bear with her weakness, which I think proceeds
29   From wayward sickness, and no grounded malice.

QUEEN ELIZABETH

      Saw you the king to-day, my Lord of Derby?

DERBY

31   But now the Duke of Buckingham and I
      Are come from visiting his majesty.

QUEEN ELIZABETH

      What likelihood of his amendment, lords?

BUCKINGHAM

      Madam, good hope; his grace speaks cheerfully.

QUEEN ELIZABETH

      God grant him health! Did you confer with him?

BUCKINGHAM

36   Ay, madam: he desires to make atonement
      Between the Duke of Gloucester and your brothers,
      And between them and my Lord Chamberlain,
      And sent to warn them to his royal presence.

QUEEN ELIZABETH

      Would all were well! but that will never be:
41   I fear our happiness is at the height.

---

20 *Countess Richmond* mother of the Earl of Richmond (later Henry VII),
now wife of Lord Stanley, Earl of Derby   29 *wayward sickness* illness not
yielding readily to treatment   31 *But now* just now   36 *atonement* reconciliation   41 *happiness . . . height* good fortune has reached its peak (any
further movement of the wheel of fortune will be down)

Enter Richard [and Lord Hastings].

RICHARD

They do me wrong, and I will not endure it!
Who is it that complains unto the king
That I (forsooth) am stern, and love them not?
By holy Paul, they love his grace but lightly
That fill his ears with such dissentious rumors.
Because I cannot flatter and look fair,
Smile in men's faces, smooth, deceive, and cog,   48
Duck with French nods and apish courtesy,   49
I must be held a rancorous enemy.
Cannot a plain man live and think no harm,
But thus his simple truth must be abused
With silken, sly, insinuating Jacks?   53

GREY

To who in all this presence speaks your grace?

RICHARD

To thee, that hast nor honesty nor grace: 55
When have I injured thee? when done thee wrong?
Or thee? or thee? or any of your faction?
A plague upon you all! His royal grace
(Whom God preserve better than you would wish!)
Cannot be quiet scarce a breathing while   60
But you must trouble him with lewd complaints.   61

QUEEN ELIZABETH

Brother of Gloucester, you mistake the matter:
The king, on his own royal disposition,   63
And not provoked by any suitor else,
Aiming (belike) at your interior hatred,
That in your outward action shows itself
Against my children, brothers, and myself,

---

48 *smooth* flatter; *cog* cheat   **49** *French nods* affected salutations   **53** *Jacks*
low-bred, worthless fellows (with play on French *Jacques*)   **55** *grace* sense of
duty or virtue (with play on the title *your grace*, l. 54)   **60** *breathing while* i.e.
long enough to catch his breath   **61** *lewd* wicked   **63–68** *The king . . . send*
(syntax confused; for 'Makes him to send' understand 'sends')   **63** *disposition* inclination

    Makes him to send, that he may learn the ground.

RICHARD

    I cannot tell : the world is grown so bad
    That wrens make prey where eagles dare not perch.
    Since every Jack became a gentleman,
    There's many a gentle person made a Jack.

QUEEN ELIZABETH

    Come, come, we know your meaning, brother
       Gloucester :
    You envy my advancement and my friends'.
    God grant we never may have need of you !

RICHARD

    Meantime, God grants that I have need of you.
    Our brother is imprisoned by your means,
    Myself disgraced, and the nobility
    Held in contempt, while great promotions
    Are daily given to ennoble those
81   That scarce, some two days since, were worth a noble.

QUEEN ELIZABETH

82   By Him that raised me to this careful height
83   From that contented hap which I enjoyed,
    I never did incense his majesty
    Against the Duke of Clarence, but have been
    An earnest advocate to plead for him.
    My lord, you do me shameful injury
88   Falsely to draw me in these vile suspects.

RICHARD

    You may deny that you were not the mean
    Of my Lord Hastings' late imprisonment.

RIVERS

    She may, my lord, for –

RICHARD

    She may, Lord Rivers ! why, who knows not so ?
    She may do more, sir, than denying that :

---

81 *noble* (1) gold coin, worth 6s. 8d., (2) nobleman   82 *careful* full of anxiety
83 *hap* fortune   88 *in* into ; *suspects* suspicions

She may help you to many fair preferments,
And then deny her aiding hand therein
And lay those honors on your high desert.
What may she not? She may – ay, marry, may she – 97

RIVERS
What, marry, may she?

RICHARD
What, marry, may she? Marry with a king,
A bachelor and a handsome stripling too:
Iwis your grandam had a worser match. 101

QUEEN ELIZABETH
My Lord of Gloucester, I have too long borne
Your blunt upbraidings and your bitter scoffs:
By heaven, I will acquaint his majesty
Of those gross taunts that oft I have endured.
I had rather be a country servant maid
Than a great queen with this condition,
To be so baited, scorned, and stormèd at: 108
  Enter old Queen Margaret [behind].
Small joy have I in being England's queen.

QUEEN MARGARET *[aside]*
And less'ned be that small, God I beseech him!
Thy honor, state, and seat is due to me. 111

She should be Queen

RICHARD
What? Threat you me with telling of the king?
[Tell him, and spare not. Look, what I have said]
I will avouch 't in presence of the king:
I dare adventure to be sent to th' Tow'r.
'Tis time to speak: my pains are quite forgot. 116

QUEEN MARGARET *[aside]*
Out, devil! I do remember them too well:
➤ Thou kill'dst my husband Henry in the Tower,
And Edward, my poor son, at Tewkesbury.

She hates him

---

97 *marry* indeed (with play on 'wed') **101** *Iwis* certainly **108** *baited*
harassed **111** *state* high rank (as queen); *seat* throne **116** *pains* efforts on
his behalf

RICHARD

Ere you were queen, ay, or your husband king,

121 I was a packhorse in his great affairs;
A weeder-out of his proud adversaries,
A liberal rewarder of his friends:
To royalize his blood I spent mine own.

QUEEN MARGARET *[aside]*

Ay, and much better blood than his or thine.

RICHARD

126 In all which time you and your husband Grey
Were factious for the house of Lancaster;
And, Rivers, so were you. Was not your husband
In Margaret's battle at Saint Albans slain?
Let me put in your minds, if you forget,
What you have been ere this, and what you are;
Withal, what I have been, and what I am.

QUEEN MARGARET *[aside]*

A murd'rous villain, and so still thou art.

RICHARD

134 Poor Clarence did forsake his father, Warwick;
Ay, and forswore himself (which Jesu pardon!) –

QUEEN MARGARET *[aside]*

Which God revenge!

RICHARD

To fight on Edward's party for the crown;

138 And for his meed, poor lord, he is mewèd up.
I would to God my heart were flint like Edward's,
Or Edward's soft and pitiful like mine:
I am too childish-foolish for this world.

QUEEN MARGARET *[aside]*

Hie thee to hell for shame, and leave this world,

143 Thou cacodemon! there thy kingdom is.

---

121 *packhorse* beast of burden, drudge   126–29 *husband . . . Saint Albans*
(the queen's first husband, Sir John Grey, was killed at the battle of Saint
Albans fighting against the Yorkists)   134 *father, Warwick* (Clarence tem-
porarily went over to the Lancastrians to marry Warwick's daughter, Isabel
Nevil)   138 *meed* reward; *mewèd up* imprisoned   143 *cacodemon* evil spirit

RIVERS

> My Lord of Gloucester, in those busy days
> Which here you urge to prove us enemies,
> We followed then our lord, our sovereign king.
> So should we you, if you should be our king.

RICHARD

> If I should be? I had rather be a pedlar:
> Far be it from my heart, the thought thereof!

QUEEN ELIZABETH

> As little joy, my lord, as you suppose
> You should enjoy, were you this country's king –
> As little joy you may suppose in me
> That I enjoy, being the queen thereof.

QUEEN MARGARET [aside]

> A little joy enjoys the queen thereof;
> For I am she, and altogether joyless.
> I can no longer hold me patient.
>   [Comes forward.]
> Hear me, you wrangling pirates, that fall out
> In sharing that which you have pilled from me!   158
> Which of you trembles not that looks on me?
> If not, that I am queen, you bow like subjects,   160
> Yet that, by you deposed, you quake like rebels?
> Ah, gentle villain, do not turn away!

RICHARD

> Foul wrinklèd witch, what mak'st thou in my sight?   163

QUEEN MARGARET

> But repetition of what thou hast marred:
> That will I make before I let thee go.

RICHARD

> Wert thou not banishèd on pain of death?

QUEEN MARGARET

> I was; but I do find more pain in banishment

---

158 *pilled* plundered   160–61 *that . . . that* because . . . because   163 *mak'st thou* are you doing (but Margaret replies as if Richard had meant 'What are you making?')

Than death can yield me here by my abode.
A husband and a son thou ow'st to me –
And thou a kingdom – all of you allegiance.
This sorrow that I have, by right is yours,
And all the pleasures you usurp are mine.

RICHARD

173 The curse my noble father laid on thee
When thou didst crown his warlike brows with paper
And with thy scorns drew'st rivers from his eyes
176 And then, to dry them, gav'st the duke a clout
Steeped in the faultless blood of pretty Rutland –
His curses then, from bitterness of soul
Denounced against thee, are all fall'n upon thee;
And God, not we, hath plagued thy bloody deed.

QUEEN ELIZABETH

So just is God, to right the innocent.

HASTINGS

O, 'twas the foulest deed to slay that babe,
And the most merciless, that e'er was heard of!

RIVERS

Tyrants themselves wept when it was reported.

DORSET

No man but prophesied revenge for it.

BUCKINGHAM

Northumberland, then present, wept to see it.

QUEEN MARGARET

What? were you snarling all before I came,
Ready to catch each other by the throat,
And turn you all your hatred now on me?
Did York's dread curse prevail so much with heaven
That Henry's death, my lovely Edward's death,
Their kingdom's loss, my woeful banishment,
193 Should all but answer for that peevish brat?
Can curses pierce the clouds and enter heaven?

173–80 *The curse . . . deed* (see *3 Henry VI*, I, iv) 176 *clout* handkerchief
193 *but answer for* merely be equal to

Why then, give way, dull clouds, to my quick curses!   195
Though not by war, by surfeit die your king,
As ours by murder, to make him a king!
Edward thy son, that now is Prince of Wales,
For Edward our son, that was Prince of Wales,
Die in his youth by like untimely violence!
Thyself a queen, for me that was a queen,
Outlive thy glory, like my wretched self!
Long mayst thou live to wail thy children's death
And see another, as I see thee now,
Decked in thy rights as thou art stalled in mine!   205
Long die thy happy days before thy death,
And, after many length'ned hours of grief,
Die neither mother, wife, nor England's queen!
Rivers and Dorset, you were standers-by,   209
And so wast thou, Lord Hastings, when my son
Was stabbed with bloody daggers: God, I pray him
That none of you may live his natural age,
But by some unlooked accident cut off!

RICHARD

Have done thy charm, thou hateful with'red hag!   214

QUEEN MARGARET

And leave out thee? stay, dog, for thou shalt hear me.
If heaven have any grievous plague in store
Exceeding those that I can wish upon thee,
O, let them keep it till thy sins be ripe,
And then hurl down their indignation
On thee, the troubler of the poor world's peace!
The worm of conscience still begnaw thy soul!
Thy friends suspect for traitors while thou liv'st,
And take deep traitors for thy dearest friends!
No sleep close up that deadly eye of thine,   224
Unless it be while some tormenting dream

195 *quick* full of life   205 *stalled* installed   209–11 *Rivers ... daggers* (none
of them was present in the scene as shown in *3 Henry VI*, V, v)   214 *charm*
magic spell (Richard addresses Margaret as a witch; cf. l. 163 above)   224
deadly killing (like the eye of a basilisk; cf. I, ii, 150)

Affrights thee with a hell of ugly devils!
227 Thou elvish-marked, abortive, rooting hog!
Thou that wast sealed in thy nativity
229 The slave of nature and the son of hell!
230 Thou slander of thy heavy mother's womb!
Thou loathèd issue of thy father's loins!
Thou rag of honor! thou detested –

RICHARD
Margaret.

QUEEN MARGARET Richard!

RICHARD   Ha!

QUEEN MARGARET   I call thee not.

RICHARD
234 I cry thee mercy then; for I did think
That thou hadst called me all these bitter names.

QUEEN MARGARET
Why, so I did, but looked for no reply.
237 O, let me make the period to my curse!

RICHARD
'Tis done by me, and ends in 'Margaret.'

QUEEN ELIZABETH
Thus have you breathed your curse against yourself.

QUEEN MARGARET
240 Poor painted queen, vain flourish of my fortune!
Why strew'st thou sugar on that bottled spider
Whose deadly web ensnareth thee about?
Fool, fool! thou whet'st a knife to kill thyself.
The day will come that thou shalt wish for me
To help thee curse this poisonous bunch-backed toad.

HASTINGS
246 False-boding woman, end thy frantic curse,

---

227 *elvish-marked* marked at birth by evil fairies; *hog* (Richard's badge was a white boar) 229 *slave of nature* naturally slavish or base-minded 230 *heavy mother's womb* mother's heavy womb, or sad mother's womb 234 *cry thee mercy* beg your pardon (sarcasm) 237 *period* end (as of a sentence; cf. II, i, 44) 240 *painted queen* queen in outward show; *flourish* meaningless decoration 246 *False-boding* prophesying falsely

Lest to thy harm thou move our patience.   247

QUEEN MARGARET

Foul shame upon you ! you have all moved mine.

RIVERS

Were you well served, you would be taught your duty.

QUEEN MARGARET

To scrve mc wcll, you all should do me duty,
Teach me to be your queen, and you my subjects :
O, serve me well, and teach yourselves that duty !

DORSET

Dispute not with her ; she is lunatic.

QUEEN MARGARET

Peace, Master Marquess, you are malapert :   254
Your fire-new stamp of honor is scarce current.   255
O, that your young nobility could judge   256
What 'twere to lose it and be miserable !
They that stand high have many blasts to shake them,
And if they fall, they dash themselves to pieces.

RICHARD

Good counsel, marry ! Learn it, learn it, Marquess.

DORSET

It touches you, my lord, as much as me.

RICHARD

Ay, and much more ; but I was born so high :
Our aery buildeth in the cedar's top   263
And dallies with the wind and scorns the sun.   264

QUEEN MARGARET

And turns the sun to shade – alas ! alas !
Witness my son, now in the shade of death,
Whose bright outshining beams thy cloudy wrath
Hath in eternal darkness folded up.
Your aery buildeth in our aery's nest :

---

247 *patience* (trisyllabic)   254 *malapert* impudent   255 *Your . . . current*
your title is so new-coined that it is scarcely legal tender   256 *young nobility*
new state of honor   263 *aery* brood of young eagles   264–65 *sun . . . sun*
(double play on 'sun,' (1) as king symbol and (2) as son)

O God, that seest it, do not suffer it !
As it is won with blood, lost be it so !

BUCKINGHAM
Peace, peace, for shame ! if not, for charity.

QUEEN MARGARET
Urge neither charity nor shame to me :
[*Turning to the others*]
Uncharitably with me have you dealt,
And shamefully my hopes by you are butchered.
My charity is outrage, life my shame,
And in that shame still live my sorrow's rage !

BUCKINGHAM
Have done, have done.

QUEEN MARGARET
O princely Buckingham, I'll kiss thy hand
280   In sign of league and amity with thee :
Now fair befall thee and thy noble house !
Thy garments are not spotted with our blood,
Nor thou within the compass of my curse.

BUCKINGHAM
Nor no one here ; for curses never pass
The lips of those that breathe them in the air.

QUEEN MARGARET
286   I will not think but they ascend the sky
And there awake God's gentle-sleeping peace.
O Buckingham, take heed of yonder dog !
289   Look when he fawns he bites ; and when he bites,
His venom tooth will rankle to the death.
Have not to do with him, beware of him :
Sin, death, and hell have set their marks on him,
And all their ministers attend on him.

RICHARD
What doth she say, my Lord of Buckingham ?

BUCKINGHAM
Nothing that I respect, my gracious lord.

---

286 *not think but* believe   289 *Look when* whenever

56

QUEEN MARGARET
    What, dost thou scorn me for my gentle counsel?
    And soothe the devil that I warn thee from?
    O, but remember this another day,
    When he shall split thy very heart with sorrow,
    And say poor Margaret was a prophetess!   300
    Live each of you the subjects to his hate,
    And he to yours, and all of you to God's!   *Exit.*

BUCKINGHAM
    My hair doth stand an end to hear her curses.

RIVERS
    And so doth mine. I muse why she's at liberty.

RICHARD
    I cannot blame her. By God's holy Mother,
    She hath had too much wrong, and I repent
    My part thereof that I have done to her.

QUEEN ELIZABETH
    I never did her any to my knowledge.

RICHARD
    Yet you have all the vantage of her wrong:
    I was too hot to do somebody good   310
    That is too cold in thinking of it now.
    Marry, as for Clarence, he is well repaid;
    He is franked up to fatting for his pains –   313
    God pardon them that are the cause thereof!

RIVERS
    A virtuous and a Christianlike conclusion –
    To pray for them that have done scathe to us.   316

RICHARD
    So do I ever – *(speaks to himself)* being well advised;
    For had I cursed now, I had cursed myself.
        Enter Catesby.

CATESBY
    Madam, his majesty doth call for you;

---

310 *too hot . . . good* i.e. too eager in helping Edward to the crown   313
franked . . . fatting shut in a sty for fattening (i.e. slaughter)   316 *scathe*
injury

And for your grace ; and yours, my gracious lord.

QUEEN ELIZABETH
Catesby, I come. Lords, will you go with me ?

RIVERS
We wait upon your grace.

Exeunt all but [Richard of] Gloucester.

RICHARD
I do the wrong, and first begin to brawl.
The secret mischiefs that I set abroach
325 I lay unto the grievous charge of others.
Clarence, who I indeed have cast in darkness,
327 I do beweep to many simple gulls –
Namely, to Derby, Hastings, Buckingham –
And tell them 'tis the queen and her allies
That stir the king against the duke my brother.
Now they believe it, and withal whet me
To be revenged on Rivers, Dorset, Grey.
But then I sigh, and, with a piece of Scripture,
Tell them that God bids us do good for evil :
And thus I clothe my naked villainy
With odd old ends stol'n forth of holy writ,
And seem a saint, when most I play the devil.

Enter two Murderers.

But soft ! Here come my executioners.
How now, my hardy, stout, resolvèd mates !
340 Are you now going to dispatch this thing ?

1 . MURDERER
We are, my lord, and come to have the warrant,
That we may be admitted where he is.

RICHARD
Well thought upon ; I have it here about me :
[Gives the warrant.]
When you have done, repair to Crosby Place.
But, sirs, be sudden in the execution,
Withal obdurate, do not hear him plead ;

---

325 *lay . . . of* impute as a severe accusation against   327 *gulls* fools

58

For Clarence is well-spoken, and perhaps
May move your hearts to pity if you mark him.

1. MURDERER
Tut, tut, my lord! we will not stand to <u>prate</u>;   349
Talkers are no good doers. Be assured:
We go to use our hands, and not our tongues.

RICHARD
Your eyes drop millstones when fools' eyes fall tears.   352
I like you, lads: about your business straight.
Go, go, dispatch.

1. MURDERER   We will, my noble lord.   *[Exeunt.]*

*

Enter Clarence and Keeper.   I, iv

KEEPER
Why looks your grace so heavily to-day?

CLARENCE
O, I have passed a miserable night,
So full of fearful dreams, of ugly sights,
That, as I am a Christian faithful man,   4
I would not spend another such a night
Though 'twere to buy a world of happy days –
So full of dismal terror was the time.

KEEPER
What was your dream, my lord? I pray you tell me.

CLARENCE
Methoughts that I had broken from the Tower
And was embarked to cross to Burgundy,
And in my company my brother Gloucester,
Who from my cabin tempted me to walk
Upon the hatches: thence we looked toward England   13
And cited up a thousand heavy times,
During the wars of York and Lancaster,

---

349 *prate* talk idly, chatter   352 *fall* let fall
I, iv The Tower of London   4 *faithful* believing in religion   13 *hatches*
moveable planks forming a kind of deck

That had befall'n us. As we paced along
17 Upon the giddy footing of the hatches,
Methought that Gloucester stumblèd, and in falling
Struck me (that thought to stay him) overboard
Into the tumbling billows of the main.
O Lord! methought what pain it was to drown!
What dreadful noise of waters in mine ears!
What sights of ugly death within mine eyes!
Methoughts I saw a thousand fearful wracks;
A thousand men that fishes gnawed upon;
Wedges of gold, great anchors, heaps of pearl,
27 Inestimable stones, unvaluèd jewels,
All scatt'red in the bottom of the sea:
Some lay in dead men's skulls, and in the holes
Where eyes did once inhabit, there were crept
(As 'twere in scorn of eyes) reflecting gems,
That wooed the slimy bottom of the deep
And mocked the dead bones that lay scatt'red by.

KEEPER
Had you such leisure in the time of death
To gaze upon these secrets of the deep?

CLARENCE
Methought I had; and often did I strive
37 To yield the ghost; but still the envious flood
Stopped in my soul, and would not let it forth
To find the empty, vast, and wand'ring air,
40 But smothered it within my panting bulk,
Who almost burst to belch it in the sea.

KEEPER
Awaked you not in this sore agony?

CLARENCE
No, no, my dream was lengthened after life.
O, then, began the tempest to my soul!
I passed (methought) the melancholy flood,

17 *giddy footing* foothold producing dizziness   27 *Inestimable . . . jewels* i.e.
precious stones without number and costly ornaments (jewels) beyond price
37 *yield the ghost* i.e. die; *still* always   40 *bulk* body

With that sour ferryman which poets write of,   46
Unto the kingdom of perpetual night.
The first that there did greet my stranger soul   48
Was my great father-in-law, renownèd Warwick,
Who spake aloud, 'What scourge for perjury
Can this dark monarchy afford false Clarence?'
And so he vanished. Then came wand'ring by
A shadow like an angel, with bright hair   53
Dabbled in blood, and he shrieked out aloud,
'Clarence is come – false, fleeting, perjured Clarence,   55
That stabbed me in the field by Tewkesbury:
Seize on him, Furies, take him unto torment!'
With that (methoughts) a legion of foul fiends
Environed me, and howlèd in mine ears
Such hideous cries that with the very noise
I, trembling, waked, and for a season after
Could not believe but that I was in hell,
Such terrible impression made my dream.

KEEPER

No marvel, lord, though it affrighted you;
I am afraid (methinks) to hear you tell it.

CLARENCE

Ah, keeper, keeper, I have done these things
(That now give evidence against my soul)
For Edward's sake, and see how he requites me!
O God! if my deep pray'rs cannot appease thee,
But thou wilt be avenged on my misdeeds,
Yet execute thy wrath in me alone:
O, spare my guiltless wife and my poor children!
Keeper, I prithee sit by me awhile.
My soul is heavy, and I fain would sleep.   74

KEEPER

I will, my lord. God give your grace good rest!
        [Clarence sleeps.]

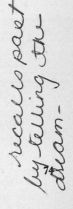

recalls past by telling the dream —

he doesn't realise this going to die

---

46 *ferryman* Charon   48 *stranger* newly arrived   53 *A shadow* i.e. Edward,
Prince of Wales, son of Henry VI   55 *fleeting* unstable   74 *My soul ... sleep*
(an omen of disaster)

Enter Brakenbury, the Lieutenant.

BRAKENBURY

76 Sorrow breaks seasons and reposing hours,
    Makes the night morning and the noontide night:
    Princes have but their titles for their glories,
    An outward honor for an inward toil;

80 And for unfelt imaginations
    They often feel a world of restless cares;
    So that between their titles and low name
    There's nothing differs but the outward fame.

Enter two Murderers.

1. MURDERER Ho! who's here?

BRAKENBURY
    What wouldst thou, fellow? and how cam'st thou hither?

1. MURDERER I would speak with Clarence, and I came
    hither on my legs.

BRAKENBURY What, so brief?

2. MURDERER 'Tis better, sir, than to be tedious. Let
    him see our commission, and talk no more.

    [Brakenbury] reads [it].

BRAKENBURY
    I am, in this, commanded to deliver

→   The noble Duke of Clarence to your hands.
    I will not reason what is meant hereby,

94 Because I will be guiltless from the meaning.
    There lies the duke asleep, and there the keys.
    I'll to the king and signify to him
    That thus I have resigned to you my charge.

1. MURDERER You may, sir; 'tis a point of wisdom. Fare
    you well.   *Exit [Brakenbury with Keeper].*

2. MURDERER What? Shall I stab him as he sleeps?

1. MURDERER No. He'll say 'twas done cowardly when
    he wakes.

---

76 *reposing hours* i.e. hours proper to sleep   80 *for unfelt imaginations* for the sake of imaginary and unreal gratifications (Dr Johnson)   94 *will be* wish to be

2. MURDERER Why, he shall never wake until the great
Judgment Day.

1. MURDERER Why, then he'll say we stabbed him sleeping.

2. MURDERER The urging of that word 'judgment' hath
bred a kind of remorse in me.

1. MURDERER What? Art thou afraid?

2. MURDERER Not to kill him, having a warrant; but to
be damned for killing him, from the which no warrant   *110*
can defend me.

1. MURDERER I thought thou hadst been resolute.

2. MURDERER So I am – to let him live.

1. MURDERER I'll back to the Duke of Gloucester and
tell him so.

2. MURDERER Nay, I prithee stay a little. I hope this pas-   *116*
sionate humor of mine will change. It was wont to hold
me but while one tells twenty.

1. MURDERER How dost thou feel thyself now?

2. MURDERER Faith, some certain dregs of conscience
are yet within me.

1. MURDERER Remember our reward when the deed's
done.

2. MURDERER Zounds, he dies! I had forgot the reward.

1. MURDERER Where's thy conscience now?

2. MURDERER O, in the Duke of Gloucester's purse.

1. MURDERER When he opens his purse to give us our
reward, thy conscience flies out.

2. MURDERER 'Tis no matter; let it go. There's few or
none will entertain it.

1. MURDERER What if it come to thee again?   *130*

2. MURDERER I'll not meddle with it; it makes a man a
coward. A man cannot steal, but it accuseth him; a man
cannot swear, but it checks him; a man cannot lie with
his neighbor's wife, but it detects him. 'Tis a blushing
shame-faced spirit that mutinies in a man's bosom. It

116 passionate compassionate

63

fills a man full of obstacles. It made me once restore a purse of gold that (by chance) I found. It beggars any man that keeps it. It is turned out of towns and cities for a dangerous thing, and every man that means to live well endeavors to trust to himself and live without it.

1 . MURDERER Zounds, 'tis even now at my elbow, persuading me not to kill the duke.

2 . MURDERER Take the devil in thy mind, and believe him not. He would insinuate with thee but to make thee sigh.

1 . MURDERER I am strong-framed; he cannot prevail with me.

2 . MURDERER Spoke like a tall man that respects thy reputation. Come, shall we fall to work?

1 . MURDERER Take him on the costard with the hilts of thy sword, and then throw him into the malmsey butt in the next room.

2 . MURDERER O excellent device! and make a sop of him.

1 . MURDERER Soft! he wakes.

2 . MURDERER Strike!

1 . MURDERER No, we'll reason with him.

CLARENCE
Where art thou, keeper? Give me a cup of wine.

2 . MURDERER
You shall have wine enough, my lord, anon.

CLARENCE
In God's name, what art thou?

1 . MURDERER
A man, as you are.

CLARENCE
But not as I am, royal.

1 . MURDERER
Nor you as we are, loyal.

143–44 *Take . . . not* call on the devil's aid and pay no heed to conscience (?) or, trap the devil conscience in your reason and pay no heed to him (?)   144 *insinuate* ingratiate himself   147 *tall* valiant   149 *costard* head   152 *sop* wafer floated in a cup of wine

64

CLARENCE
Thy voice is thunder, but thy looks are humble.

1. MURDERER
My voice is now the king's, my looks mine own.

CLARENCE
How darkly and how deadly dost thou speak!   164
Your eyes do menace me. Why look you pale?
Who sent you hither? Wherefore do you come?

BOTH To, to, to –

CLARENCE
To murder me?

BOTH Ay, ay.

CLARENCE
You scarcely have the hearts to tell me so,
And therefore cannot have the hearts to do it.
Wherein, my friends, have I offended you?

1. MURDERER
Offended us you have not, but the king.

CLARENCE
I shall be reconciled to him again.

2. MURDERER
Never, my lord; therefore prepare to die.

CLARENCE
Are you drawn forth among a world of men   176
To slay the innocent? What is my offense?
Where is the evidence that doth accuse me?
What lawful quest have given their verdict up   179
Unto the frowning judge? or who pronounced
The bitter sentence of poor Clarence' death
Before I be convict by course of law?
To threaten me with death is most unlawful:
I charge you, as you hope [to have redemption
By Christ's dear blood shed for our grievous sins,]
That you depart, and lay no hands on me.

---

164 *deadly* threatening death   176 *drawn . . . men* i.e. specially chosen
among all mankind   179 *quest* jury

187   The deed you undertake is <u>damnable</u>.

1. MURDERER
What we will do, we do upon command.

2. MURDERER
And he that hath commanded is our king.

CLARENCE
Erroneous vassals! the great King of Kings
Hath in the table of his law commanded
That thou shalt do no murder. Will you then
Spurn at his edict, and fulfil a man's?
Take heed; for he holds vengeance in his hand
To hurl upon their heads that break his law.

2. MURDERER
And that same vengeance doth he hurl on thee
For false forswearing and for murder too:
Thou didst receive the sacrament to fight
In quarrel of the house of Lancaster.

1. MURDERER
And like a traitor to the name of God
Didst break that vow, and with thy treacherous blade
Unrip'st the bowels of thy sov'reign's son.

2. MURDERER
Whom thou wast sworn to cherish and defend.

1. MURDERER
How canst thou urge God's dreadful law to us
205   When thou hast broke it in such <u>dear degree</u>?

CLARENCE
Alas! for whose sake did I that ill deed?
For Edward, for my brother, for his sake.
He sends you not to murder me for this,
For in that sin he is as deep as I.
If God will be avengèd for the deed,
O, know you yet he doth it publicly!
Take not the quarrel from his pow'rful arm.

---

187 *damnable* leading to damnation (for you) 205 *dear degree* serious
measure

He needs no indirect or lawless course
To cut off those that have offended him.

1 . MURDERER
Who made thee then a bloody minister
When gallant-springing brave Plantagenet,
That princely novice, was struck dead by thee?   217

CLARENCE
My brother's love, the devil, and my rage.

1 . MURDERER
Thy brother's love, our duty, and thy faults
Provoke us hither now to slaughter thee.

CLARENCE
O, if you love my brother, hate not me :
I am his brother, and I love him well.
If you are hired for meed, go back again,   *(irony)*   223
And I will send you to my brother Gloucester,
Who shall reward you better for my life
Than Edward will for tidings of my death.

2 . MURDERER
You are deceived. Your brother Gloucester hates you.

CLARENCE
O, no, he loves me and he holds me dear :
Go you to him from me.

1 . MURDERER   Ay, so we will.

CLARENCE
Tell him, when that our princely father York
Blessed his three sons with his victorious arm
[And charged us from his soul to love each other,]
He little thought of this divided friendship :
Bid Gloucester think of this, and he will weep.

1 . MURDERER
Ay, millstones, as he lessoned us to weep.

CLARENCE
O, do not slander him, for he is kind.   236

217 *novice* one just beginning his duties   223 *meed* reward   236 *kind* (1)
with feelings natural to a brother, (2) good

1. MURDERER

237   Right as snow in harvest. Come, you deceive yourself;
        'Tis he that sends us to destroy you here.

CLARENCE

        It cannot be, for he bewept my fortune,
        And hugged me in his arms, and swore with sobs
        That he would labor my delivery.

1. MURDERER

        Why so he doth, when he delivers you
        From this earth's thraldom to the joys of heaven.

2. MURDERER

        Make peace with God, for you must die, my lord.

CLARENCE

        Have you that holy feeling in your souls
        To counsel me to make my peace with God,
        And are you yet to your own souls so blind
        That you will war with God by murd'ring me?
        O, sirs, consider, they that set you on

250   To do this deed will hate you for the deed.

2. MURDERER

        What shall we do?

CLARENCE   Relent, and save your souls.
        Which of you, if you were a prince's son,
        Being pent from liberty, as I am now,
        If two such murderers as yourselves came to you,
        Would not entreat for life?

1. MURDERER

        Relent? No: 'tis cowardly and womanish.

CLARENCE

        Not to relent is beastly, savage, devilish.
        My friend [to Second Murderer], I spy some pity in thy
            looks.
        O, if thine eye be not a flatterer,

260   Come thou on my side, and entreat for me
        As you would beg, were you in my distress.

237 *Right as* just as much as

A begging prince what beggar pities not ?

2 . MURDERER
Look behind you, my lord !

1 . MURDERER
Take that ! and that !*(Stabs him.)* If all this will not do,
I'll drown you in the malmsey butt within.
Exit [with the body].

2 . MURDERER
A bloody deed, and desperately dispatched !
How fain (like Pilate) would I wash my hands
Of this most grievous murder !
Enter First Murderer.

1 . MURDERER
How now ? What mean'st thou that thou help'st me not ?
By heavens, the duke shall know how slack you have been.   270

2 . MURDERER
I would he knew that I had saved his brother !
Take thou the fee and tell him what I say,
For I repent me that the duke is slain.   *Exit.*

1 . MURDERER
So do not I. Go, coward as thou art.
Well, I'll go hide the body in some hole
Till that the duke give order for his burial ;
And when I have my meed, I will away,
For this will out, and then I must not stay.   *Exit.* 278

*

Flourish. Enter the King [Edward], sick, the   II, i
Queen, Lord Marquess Dorset, [Grey,] Rivers,
Hastings, Catesby, [and] Buckingham.

KING EDWARD
Why, so : now have I done a good day's work.
You peers, continue this united league.

---

278 *this will out* i.e. murder will out (proverbial)
II, i The royal palace

I every day expect an embassage
From my Redeemer to redeem me hence ;
And more in peace my soul shall part to heaven,
Since I have made my friends at peace on earth.
Hastings and Rivers, take each other's hand ;
8 Dissemble not your hatred, swear your love.

RIVERS
By heaven, my soul is purged from grudging hate,
And with my hand I seal my true heart's love.

HASTINGS
So thrive I as I truly swear the like !

KING EDWARD
12 Take heed you dally not before your king,
Lest he that is the supreme King of Kings
Confound your hidden falsehood and award
Either of you to be the other's end.

HASTINGS
So prosper I as I swear perfect love !

RIVERS
And I as I love Hastings with my heart !

KING EDWARD
Madam, yourself is not exempt from this ;
Nor you, son Dorset ; Buckingham, nor you :
20 You have been factious one against the other.
Wife, love Lord Hastings, let him kiss your hand,
And what you do, do it unfeignedly.

QUEEN ELIZABETH
There, Hastings. I will never more remember
Our former hatred, so thrive I and mine !

KING EDWARD
Dorset, embrace him ; Hastings, love Lord Marquess.

DORSET
This interchange of love, I here protest,
Upon my part shall be inviolable.

---

8 *Dissemble . . . hatred* do not hide hatred under a false appearance (of love)
12 *dally* trifle

reuniting everyone

HASTINGS

    And so swear I.

KING EDWARD

    Now, princely Buckingham, seal thou this league
    With thy embracements to my wife's allies,
    And make me happy in your unity.

BUCKINGHAM *[to the Queen]*

    Whenever Buckingham doth turn his hate   32
    Upon your grace, but with all duteous love
    Doth cherish you and yours, God punish me
    With hate in those where I expect most love!
    When I have most need to employ a friend,
    And most assurèd that he is a friend,
    Deep, hollow, treacherous, and full of guile
    Be he unto me! This do I beg of God,
    When I am cold in love to you or yours.
        Embrace.

KING EDWARD

    A pleasing cordial, princely Buckingham,
    Is this thy vow unto my sickly heart.
    There wanteth now our brother Gloucester here
    To make the blessèd period of this peace.   44

BUCKINGHAM

    And in good time,
    Here comes Sir Richard Ratcliffe and the duke.
        Enter [Sir Richard] Ratcliffe and [Richard, Duke of]
        Gloucester.

RICHARD

    Good morrow to my sovereign king and queen;
    And, princely peers, a happy time of day!

KING EDWARD

    Happy indeed, as we have spent the day:
    Gloucester, we have done deeds of charity,
    Made peace of enmity, fair love of hate,

32–35 *Whenever . . . love* (construction incoherent; for 'but,' l. 33, understand 'nor')   44 *period* conclusion (cf. I, iii, 237)

Between these swelling wrong-incensèd peers.

RICHARD

A blessèd labor, my most sovereign lord:
Among this princely heap, if any here
By false intelligence or wrong surmise
Hold me a foe —
If I unwittingly, or in my rage,
Have aught committed that is hardly borne
By any in this presence, I desire

60   To reconcile me to his friendly peace.
'Tis death to me to be at enmity:
I hate it, and desire all good men's love.
First, madam, I entreat true peace of you,
Which I will purchase with my duteous service;
Of you, my noble cousin Buckingham,
If ever any grudge were lodged between us;

67   Of you, and you, Lord Rivers, and of Dorset,
68   That, all without desert, have frowned on me;
Dukes, earls, lords, gentlemen — indeed, of all.
I do not know that Englishman alive
With whom my soul is any jot at odds
More than the infant that is born to-night.
I thank my God for my humility.

QUEEN ELIZABETH

A holy day shall this be kept hereafter:
I would to God all strifes were well compounded.
My sovereign lord, I do beseech your highness
To take our brother Clarence to your grace.

RICHARD

Why, madam, have I off'red love for this,
79   To be so flouted in this royal presence?
Who knows not that the gentle duke is dead?
They all start.

60 *reconcile ... peace* i.e. bring myself into friendly relations with him   67 *of Dorset* ('Lord' understood)   68 *all without desert* entirely without my having deserved it   72 *More ... infant* i.e. more than that infant's soul is 79 *flouted* mocked at

[handwritten top margin: R makes ct deem as (accuses Liz) of pretending not to know - ironic]

You do him injury to scorn his corse.   81

KING EDWARD
    Who knows not he is dead ? Who knows he is ?

QUEEN ELIZABETH
    All-seeing heaven, what a world is this !

BUCKINGHAM
    Look I so pale, Lord Dorset, as the rest ?

DORSET
    Ay, my good lord ; and no man in the presence   85
    But his red color hath forsook his cheeks.

KING EDWARD
    Is Clarence dead ? The order was reversed.

RICHARD
    But he (poor man) by your first order died,
    And that a wingèd Mercury did bear :   *[handwritten: done quickly]*
    Some tardy cripple bare the countermand, → *[handwritten: slowly (f. as.)]*
    That came too lag to see him burièd.   91
    God grant that some, less noble and less loyal,
    Nearer in bloody thoughts, but not in blood,
    Deserve not worse than wretched Clarence did,
    And yet go current from suspicion !   95
        Enter [Lord Stanley,] Earl of Derby.

DERBY
    A boon, my sovereign, for my service done !   96

KING EDWARD
    I prithee peace. My soul is full of sorrow.

DERBY
    I will not rise unless your highness hear me.

KING EDWARD
    Then say at once what is it thou requests.

DERBY
    The forfeit, sovereign, of my servant's life,   100
    Who slew to-day a riotous gentleman

---

81 *scorn his corse* i.e. joke about the dead   85 *presence* i.e. king's presence
91 *lag* late   95 *go . . . suspicion* are accepted (as legal tender at face value)
without question   96 *boon* favor   100 *forfeit . . . life* (the remission of the
forfeit is the boon)

[handwritten bottom margin: figure of speech (eg metaphors)
by simile
say one thing, mean something else]

73

Lately attendant on the Duke of Norfolk.

KING EDWARD

Have I a tongue to doom my brother's death,
And shall that tongue give pardon to a slave?
My brother killed no man – his fault was thought –
And yet his punishment was bitter death.
Who sued to me for him? Who (in my wrath)
Kneeled at my feet and bid me be advised?
Who spoke of brotherhood? Who spoke of love?
Who told me how the poor soul did forsake

111   The mighty Warwick and did fight for me?
Who told me, in the field at Tewkesbury,

113   When Oxford had me down, he rescuèd me
And said, 'Dear brother, live, and be a king'?
Who told me, when we both lay in the field
Frozen (almost) to death, how he did lap me
Even in his garments, and did give himself
(All thin and naked) to the numb-cold night?
All this from my remembrance brutish wrath

120   Sinfully plucked, and not a man of you
Had so much grace to put it in my mind.
But when your carters or your waiting vassals
Have done a drunken slaughter and defaced
The precious image of our dear Redeemer,
You straight are on your knees for pardon, pardon;
And I (unjustly too) must grant it you.

     [Derby rises.]

But for my brother not a man would speak,
Nor I (ungracious) speak unto myself

130   For him, poor soul! The proudest of you all
Have been beholding to him in his life;
Yet none of you would once beg for his life.
O God! I fear thy justice will take hold

---

111 *Warwick* (Clarence returned to the Yorkist side after marrying Warwick's daughter, thus perjuring himself)   113 *Oxford* (an incident neither
historical nor in *3 Henry VI*)

On me and you, and mine and yours, for this.
Come, Hastings, help me to my closet. Ah, poor Clarence!   *Exeunt some with King and Queen.*

RICHARD

This is the fruits of rashness! Marked you not
How that the guilty kindred of the queen
Looked pale when they did hear of Clarence' death?
O, they did urge it still unto the king!
God will revenge it. Come, lords, will you go
To comfort Edward with our company?   *140*

BUCKINGHAM

We wait upon your grace.   *Exeunt.*

R is a murderer
Ed feels guilty for what R did

          Enter the old Duchess of York, with the two   II, ii
          Children of Clarence [Edward and Margaret
          Plantagenet].

BOY

Good grandam, tell us, is our father dead?

DUCHESS OF YORK No, boy.

GIRL

Why do you weep so oft, and beat your breast,
And cry 'O Clarence, my unhappy son'?

BOY

Why do you look on us, and shake your head,
And call us orphans, wretches, castaways,
If that our noble father were alive?

DUCHESS OF YORK

My pretty cousins, you mistake me both.
I do lament the sickness of the king,
As loath to lose him, not your father's death:
It were lost sorrow to wail one that's lost.

BOY

Then you conclude, my grandam, he is dead.

the prevent
christopher
Clar- is indead   8

II, ii The same   8 *you . . . both* you both misunderstand me

13   The king mine uncle is too blame for it :
      God will revenge it, whom I will importune
      With earnest prayers all to that effect.

GIRL
      And so will I.

DUCHESS OF YORK
      Peace, children, peace ! The king doth love you well.
18   Incapable and shallow innocents,
      You cannot guess who caused your father's death.

BOY
      Grandam, we can ; for my good uncle Gloucester
      Told me the king, provoked to it by the queen,
22   Devised impeachments to imprison him ;
      And when my uncle told me so, he wept,
      And pitied me, and kindly kissed my cheek ;
      Bade me rely on him as on my father,
      And he would love me dearly as a child.

DUCHESS OF YORK
27   Ah, that deceit should steal such gentle shape
28   And with a virtuous visor hide deep vice !
      He is my son – ay, and therein my shame ;
      Yet from my dugs he drew not this deceit.

BOY
      Think you my uncle did dissemble, grandam ?
DUCHESS OF YORK Ay, boy.
BOY
      I cannot think it. Hark ! What noise is this ?
            Enter the Queen [Elizabeth], with her hair about
            her ears, Rivers and Dorset after her.

QUEEN ELIZABETH
      Ah, who shall hinder me to wail and weep,
      To chide my fortune, and torment myself ?
      I'll join with black despair against my soul
      And to myself become an enemy.

---

13 *too blame* blameworthy ('blame' felt as adjectival)   18 *Incapable* without
power of understanding   22 *impeachments* accusations   27 *shape* disguise
28 *visor* mask

DUCHESS OF YORK

What means this scene of rude impatience?   38

QUEEN ELIZABETH

To make an act of tragic violence.
Edward, my lord, thy son, our king, is dead!
Why grow the branches when the root is gone?
Why wither not the leaves that want their sap?
If you will live, lament; if die, be brief,
That our swift-wingèd souls may catch the king's,
Or like obedient subjects follow him
To his new kingdom of ne'er-changing night.

DUCHESS OF YORK

Ah, so much interest have I in thy sorrow
As I had title in thy noble husband.   48
I have bewept a worthy husband's death,
And lived with looking on his images;   50
But now two mirrors of his princely semblance   51
Are cracked in pieces by malignant death,
And I for comfort have but one false glass
That grieves me when I see my shame in him.
Thou art a widow; yet thou art a mother,
And hast the comfort of thy children left;
But death hath snatched my husband from mine arms
And plucked two crutches from my feeble hands,
Clarence and Edward. O, what cause have I   59
(Thine being but a moi'ty of my moan)   60
To overgo thy woes and drown thy cries!

BOY

Ah, aunt! you wept not for our father's death.
How can we aid you with our kindred tears?   63

GIRL

Our fatherless distress was left unmoaned:

38–39 *scene . . . violence* (note the playhouse imagery; cf. ll. 27–28 and III, v,
1–11) 48 *title* legal right 50 *lived with* i.e. kept myself alive by; *images* i.e.
children 51 *mirrors* i.e. Clarence and King Edward 59 *what . . . I* what a
cause I have 60 *moi'ty of my moan* half (the cause) of my grief 63 *kindred
tears* i.e. tears belonging to relatives

Your widow-dolor likewise be unwept!

QUEEN ELIZABETH
Give me no help in lamentation;
67   I am not barren to bring forth complaints.
68   All springs reduce their currents to mine eyes,
That I, being governed by the watery moon,
May send forth plenteous tears to drown the world.
Ah for my husband, for my dear lord Edward!

CHILDREN
Ah for our father, for our dear lord Clarence!

DUCHESS OF YORK
Alas for both, both mine, Edward and Clarence!

QUEEN ELIZABETH
What stay had I but Edward? and he's gone.

CHILDREN
What stay had we but Clarence? and he's gone.

DUCHESS OF YORK
What stays had I but they? and they are gone.

QUEEN ELIZABETH
Was never widow had so dear a loss.

CHILDREN
Were never orphans had so dear a loss.

DUCHESS OF YORK
Was never mother had so dear a loss.
Alas! I am the mother of these griefs:
81   Their woes are parcelled, mine is general.
She for an Edward weeps, and so do I;
I for a Clarence weep, so doth not she:
These babes for Clarence weep, [and so do I;
I for an Edward weep,] so do not they.
Alas, you three on me, threefold distressed,
Pour all your tears! I am your sorrow's nurse,
88   And I will pamper it with lamentation.

67 *I ... complaints* I have a full capacity for uttering complaints   68 *reduce*
bring (as to a reservoir)   81 *parcelled* particular to each one   88 *pamper ...*
lamentation i.e. feed sorrow with sorrow

DORSET

> Comfort, dear mother ; God is much displeased
> That you take with unthankfulness his doing.
> In common worldly things 'tis called ungrateful
> With dull unwillingness to repay a debt
> Which with a bounteous hand was kindly lent ;
> Much more to be thus opposite with heaven   94
> For it requires the royal debt it lent you.   95

RIVERS

> Madam, bethink you like a careful mother
> Of the young prince your son. Send straight for him ;
> Let him be crowned ; in him your comfort lives.
> Drown desperate sorrow in dead Edward's grave
> And plant your joys in living Edward's throne.
> > *Enter Richard, Buckingham, [Stanley Earl of]*
> > *Derby, Hastings, and Ratcliffe.*

RICHARD

> Sister, have comfort. All of us have cause
> To wail the dimming of our shining star ;
> But none can help our harms by wailing them.
> Madam, my mother, I do cry you mercy ;
> I did not see your grace. Humbly on my knee
> I crave your blessing.

DUCHESS OF YORK

> God bless thee, and put meekness in thy breast,
> Love, charity, obedience, and true duty !

RICHARD

> Amen ! – *[aside]* and make me die a good old man !
> That is the butt-end of a mother's blessing ;
> I marvel that her grace did leave it out.

BUCKINGHAM

> You cloudy princes and heart-sorrowing peers
> That bear this heavy mutual load of moan,   113
> Now cheer each other in each other's love.

---

94 *opposite with* opposed to   95 *For* because   113 *load of moan* i.e. weight or
cause of lamentation

Though we have spent our harvest of this king,
We are to reap the harvest of his son.
117   The broken rancor of your high-swol'n hates,
118   But lately splintered, knit, and joined together,
Must gently be preserved, cherished, and kept.
120   Me seemeth good that with some little train
121   Forthwith from Ludlow the young prince be fet
Hither to London, to be crowned our king.

RIVERS
Why with some little train, my Lord of Buckingham?

BUCKINGHAM
124   Marry, my lord, lest by a multitude
The new-healed wound of malice should break out,
Which would be so much the more dangerous
127   By how much the estate is green and yet ungoverned.
Where every horse bears his commanding rein
And may direct his course as please himself,
As well the fear of harm as harm apparent,
In my opinion, ought to be prevented.

RICHARD
I hope the king made peace with all of us;
And the compact is firm and true in me.

RIVERS
And so in me; and so (I think) in all.
Yet, since it is but green, it should be put
To no apparent likelihood of breach,
Which haply by much company might be urged.
Therefore I say with noble Buckingham
That it is meet so few should fetch the prince.

HASTINGS
And so say I.

117–19 *The broken . . . kept* (meaning confused; understand 'broken rancor'
as implying 'new-found amity')   118 *splintered* set in splints   120 *Me
seemeth* it seems to me   121 *Ludlow* town in south Shropshire; *fet* fetched
124 *multitude* large train or following   127 *estate is green* administration of
government is untried

RICHARD
    Then be it so ; and go we to determine
    Who they shall be that straight shall post to Ludlow.
    Madam, and you, my sister, will you go
    To give your censures in this business ?   144
[BOTH
    With all our hearts.]
                    Exeunt. Manent Buckingham and Richard.
BUCKINGHAM
    My lord, whoever journeys to the prince,
    For God sake let not us two stay at home ;
    For by the way I'll sort occasion,   148
    As index to the story we late talked of,   149
    To part the queen's proud kindred from the prince.
RICHARD
    My other self, my counsel's consistory,   151
    My oracle, my prophet, my dear cousin,
    I, as a child, will go by thy direction.
    Toward Ludlow then, for we'll not stay behind. *Exeunt.*

                            *

             Enter one Citizen at one door and another at the other. II, iii
1. CITIZEN
    Good morrow, neighbor. Whither away so fast ?
2. CITIZEN
    I promise you, I scarcely know myself.
    Hear you the news abroad ?
1. CITIZEN   Yes, that the king is dead.
2. CITIZEN
    Ill news, by'r Lady – seldom comes the better :   4
    I fear, I fear 'twill prove a giddy world.   5

144 *censures* judgments   148 *sort occasion* make an opportunity   149 *index*
prologue   151 *consistory* council chamber
II, iii A London street   4 *seldom . . . better* (times are bad) but are likely to
be worse (proverbial)   5 *giddy* inconstant or mad

Enter another Citizen.

3. CITIZEN
Neighbors, God speed!

1. CITIZEN   Give you good morrow, sir.

3. CITIZEN
Doth the news hold of good King Edward's death?

2. CITIZEN
Ay, sir, it is too true. God help the while!

3. CITIZEN
Then, masters, look to see a troublous world.

1. CITIZEN
No, no! By God's good grace his son shall reign.

3. CITIZEN
Woe to that land that's governed by a child!

2. CITIZEN
12   In him there is a hope of government,
Which, in his nonage, council under him,
And, in his full and ripened years, himself,
No doubt shall then, and till then, govern well.

1. CITIZEN
So stood the state when Henry the Sixth
Was crowned in Paris but at nine months old.

3. CITIZEN
18   Stood the state so? No, no, good friends, God wot!
For then this land was famously enriched
20   With politic grave counsel; then the king
Had virtuous uncles to protect his grace.

1. CITIZEN
Why, so hath this, both by his father and mother.

3. CITIZEN
Better it were they all came by his father,
Or by his father there were none at all;
For emulation who shall now be nearest

12–15 *In him . . . well* (confused construction: there is hope for the land; for
one who in his minority governs wisely with the aid of counsel will in his
maturity govern well in his own person)   18 *wot* knows   20 *counsel* pro-
fessional advisers

Will touch us all too near, if God prevent not.
O, full of danger is the Duke of Gloucester,
And the queen's sons and brothers haught and proud;   28
And were they to be ruled, and not to rule,
This sickly land might solace as before.   30

1. CITIZEN
Come, come, we fear the worst. All will be well.

3. CITIZEN
When clouds are seen, wise men put on their cloaks;   32
When great leaves fall, then winter is at hand;
When the sun sets, who doth not look for night?
Untimely storms makes men expect a dearth.
All may be well; but if God sort it so,   36
'Tis more than we deserve or I expect.

2. CITIZEN
Truly, the hearts of men are full of fear:
You cannot reason (almost) with a man   39
That looks not heavily and full of dread.

3. CITIZEN
Before the days of change, still is it so.
By a divine instinct men's minds mistrust
Ensuing danger; as by proof we see
The water swell before a boist'rous storm.
But leave it all to God. Whither away?

2. CITIZEN
Marry, we were sent for to the justices.

3. CITIZEN
And so was I. I'll bear you company.   *Exeunt.*

28 *haught* haughty   30 *solace* be happy   32–35 *When . . . dearth* (a series of
'moral sentences' in the manner of Senecan tragedy)   36 *sort* dispose   39
You . . . man i.e. there is almost no man with whom you can reason

II, iv   *Enter [the] Archbishop [of York], [the] young*
               [Duke of] York, the Queen [Elizabeth], and the
               Duchess [of York].

ARCHBISHOP

1   Last night, I hear, they lay at Stony Stratford;

2   And at Northampton they do rest to-night;
    To-morrow, or next day, they will be here.

DUCHESS OF YORK

    I long with all my heart to see the prince:
    I hope he is much grown since last I saw him.

QUEEN ELIZABETH

    But I hear no. They say my son of York
    Has almost overta'en him in his growth.

YORK

    Ay, mother; but I would not have it so.

DUCHESS OF YORK

    Why, my good cousin? it is good to grow.

YORK

    Grandam, one night as we did sit at supper,
    My uncle Rivers talked how I did grow
    More than my brother. 'Ay,' quoth my uncle
        Gloucester,

13   'Small herbs have grace; great weeds do grow apace.'
    And since, methinks, I would not grow so fast,
    Because sweet flow'rs are slow and weeds make haste.

DUCHESS OF YORK

    Good faith, good faith, the saying did not hold

17   In him that did object the same to thee:
    He was the wretched'st thing when he was young,
    So long a-growing and so leisurely

20   That, if his rule were true, he should be gracious.

II, iv The royal palace   **1** *Stony Stratford* town in Buckinghamshire   **2**
Northampton town in Northamptonshire (Historically the order of these
two towns is correct, though dramatically the order is difficult since Stony
Stratford is closer to London than Northampton is – see l. 3. The quartos
reverse the order.)   **13** *grace* beneficent virtue   **17** *object* urge   **20** *gracious*
(playing on *grace*, l. 13)

ARCHBISHOP
And so no doubt he is, my gracious madam.

DUCHESS OF YORK
I hope he is ; but yet let mothers doubt.

YORK
Now, by my troth, if I had been rememb'red,   23
I could have given my uncle's grace a flout   24
To touch his growth nearer than he touched mine.

DUCHESS OF YORK
How, my young York ? I prithee let me hear it.

YORK
Marry (they say) my uncle grew so fast
That he could gnaw a crust at two hours old :
'Twas full two years ere I could get a tooth.
Grandam, this would have been a biting jest.   30

DUCHESS OF YORK
I prithee, pretty York, who told thee this ?

YORK
Grandam, his nurse.

DUCHESS OF YORK
His nurse ? Why, she was dead ere thou wast born.

YORK
If 'twere not she, I cannot tell who told me.

QUEEN ELIZABETH
A parlous boy ! Go to, you are too shrewd.   35

DUCHESS OF YORK
Good madam, be not angry with the child.

QUEEN ELIZABETH
Pitchers have ears.   37
        Enter a Messenger.

ARCHBISHOP
Here comes a messenger. What news ?

MESSENGER
Such news, my lord, as grieves me to report.

---

23 *troth* faith ; *been rememb'red* considered   **24** *flout* scoff   **30** *biting* (note play on 'teeth' in ll. 28–29)   **35** *parlous* cunning   **37** *Pitchers have ears* (proverbial : little pitchers have wide ears – said of children)

QUEEN ELIZABETH
  How doth the prince?
MESSENGER   Well, madam, and in health.
DUCHESS OF YORK
  What is thy news?
MESSENGER
42 Lord Rivers and Lord Grey are sent to Pomfret,
43 And with them Sir Thomas Vaughan, prisoners.
DUCHESS OF YORK
  Who hath committed them?
MESSENGER   The mighty dukes,
  Gloucester and Buckingham.
ARCHBISHOP   For what offense?
MESSENGER
46 The sum of all I can I have disclosed.
  Why or for what the nobles were committed
  Is all unknown to me, my gracious lord.
QUEEN ELIZABETH
  Ay me! I see the ruin of my house.
  The tiger now hath seized the gentle hind;
51 Insulting tyranny begins to jut
52 Upon the innocent and aweless throne:
  Welcome destruction, blood, and massacre!
54 I see (as in a map) the end of all.
DUCHESS OF YORK
  Accursèd and unquiet wrangling days,
  How many of you have mine eyes beheld!
57 My husband lost his life to get the crown,
  And often up and down my sons were tossed
  For me to joy and weep their gain and loss;
  And being seated, and domestic broils
  Clean overblown, themselves the conquerors

---

42 *Pomfret* castle in Yorkshire   43 *Vaughan* (dissyllabic throughout)   46
can know   51 *jut* encroach upon   52 *aweless* inspiring no awe   54 *map*
(figuratively) something representing (future) events in epitome   57–63
My husband...self (note the 'wheel of fortune' theme underlying these lines)

Make war upon themselves, brother to brother,
Blood to blood, self against self. O preposterous   63
And frantic outrage, end thy damnèd spleen,   64
Or let me die, to look on death no more!

QUEEN ELIZABETH
Come, come, my boy; we will to sanctuary.   66
Madam, farewell.

DUCHESS OF YORK Stay, I will go with you.

QUEEN ELIZABETH
You have no cause.

ARCHBISHOP [to the Queen] My gracious lady, go,
And thither bear your treasure and your goods.
For my part, I'll resign unto your grace
The seal I keep; and so betide to me
As well I tender you and all of yours!   72
Go, I'll conduct you to the sanctuary.   Exeunt.

*

The trumpets sound. Enter young Prince   III, i
[Edward of Wales], the Dukes of Gloucester and
Buckingham, Lord Cardinal [Bourchier, Catesby,]
with others.

BUCKINGHAM
Welcome, sweet prince, to London, to your chamber.   1

RICHARD
Welcome, dear cousin, my thoughts' sovereign:
The weary way hath made you melancholy.

PRINCE EDWARD
No, uncle; but our crosses on the way   4
Have made it tedious, wearisome, and heavy.
I want more uncles here to welcome me.   6

---

63 *preposterous* inverting the natural order   64 *spleen* malice   66 *sanctuary*
the cathedral precincts in which civil law was powerless   72 *tender* care for
III, i A London street   1 *chamber* (London was known as *camera regis* or
king's chamber)   4 *crosses* annoyances (play on *melancholy*, l. 3)   6 *want*
(1) am lacking in, (2) desire (cf. l. 12)

Queen at Sanctuary to stay away from R.

he tells ed that their uncles are bad

RICHARD

Sweet prince, the untainted virtue of your years
Hath not yet dived into the world's deceit:
Nor more can you distinguish of a man
Than of his outward show, which, God he knows,
Seldom or never jumpeth with the heart.
Those uncles which you want were dangerous;
Your grace attended to their sug'red words
But looked not on the poison of their hearts:
God keep you from them, and from such false friends!

PRINCE EDWARD

God keep me from false friends! – but they were none.

RICHARD

My lord, the Mayor of London comes to greet you.
        Enter Lord Mayor [and his Train].

LORD MAYOR

God bless your grace with health and happy days!

PRINCE EDWARD

I thank you, good my lord, and thank you all.
        [Mayor and his Train stand aside.]
I thought my mother and my brother York
Would long ere this have met us on the way.
Fie, what a slug is Hastings that he comes not
To tell us whether they will come or no!
        Enter Lord Hastings.

BUCKINGHAM

And, in good time, here comes the sweating lord.

PRINCE EDWARD

Welcome, my lord. What, will our mother come?

HASTINGS

On what occasion God he knows, not I,
The queen your mother and your brother York
Have taken sanctuary. The tender prince
Would fain have come with me to meet your grace,

11 *jumpeth* accords   22 *slug* lazy fellow (sluggard)   26 *On what occasion* for
what reason

But by his mother was perforce withheld.   30

BUCKINGHAM

 Fie, what an indirect and peevish course   31
 Is this of hers ! Lord Cardinal, will your grace
 Persuade the queen to send the Duke of York
 Unto his princely brother presently ?   34
 If she deny, Lord Hastings, go with him
 And from her jealous arms pluck him perforce.

CARDINAL BOURCHIER

 My Lord of Buckingham, if my weak oratory
 Can from his mother win the Duke of York,
 Anon expect him here ; but if she be obdurate
 To mild entreaties, God in heaven forbid
 We should infringe the holy privilege
 Of blessèd sanctuary ! Not for all this land
 Would I be guilty of so deep a sin.

BUCKINGHAM

 You are too senseless-obstinate, my lord,
 Too ceremonious and traditional.
 Weigh it but with the grossness of this age,   45
 You break not sanctuary in seizing him :   46
 The benefit thereof is always granted
 To those whose dealings have deserved the place
 And those who have the wit to claim the place.
 This prince hath neither claimed it nor deserved it,
 And therefore, in mine opinion, cannot have it.
 Then, taking him from thence that is not there,
 You break no privilege nor charter there.
 Oft have I heard of sanctuary men,
 But sanctuary children never till now.

CARDINAL BOURCHIER

 My lord, you shall overrule my mind for once.
 Come on, Lord Hastings, will you go with me ?

---

30 *perforce* forcibly   31 *indirect and peevish* devious and perverse   34
presently at once   45 *ceremonious* tied by formalities   46 *grossness* coarse-
ness or lack of refinement (in a moral sense)

[handwritten marginalia]

HASTINGS
   I go, my lord.
PRINCE EDWARD
   Good lords, make all the speedy haste you may.
                         Exeunt Cardinal and Hastings.
   Say, uncle Gloucester, if our brother come,
   Where shall we sojourn till our coronation?
RICHARD
   Where it seems best unto your royal self.
   If I may counsel you, some day or two
65 Your highness shall repose you at the Tower;
   Then where you please, and shall be thought most fit
   For your best health and recreation.
PRINCE EDWARD
68 I do not like the Tower, of any place.
   Did Julius Caesar build that place, my lord?
BUCKINGHAM
   He did, my gracious lord, begin that place,
   Which, since, succeeding ages have re-edified.
PRINCE EDWARD
   Is it upon record, or else reported
   Successively from age to age, he built it?
BUCKINGHAM
   Upon record, my gracious lord.
PRINCE EDWARD
   But say, my lord, it were not regist'red,
   Methinks the truth should live from age to age,
   As 'twere retailed to all posterity,
   Even to the general all-ending day.
RICHARD *[aside]*
   So wise so young, they say, do never live long.
PRINCE EDWARD
   What say you, uncle?

65 *Tower* the Tower of London (associated in the prince's mind with imprisonment; cf. I, i, 45)   68 *of any place* of all places

90

RICHARD

I say, without characters fame lives long. 81
[Aside]
Thus, like the formal Vice, Iniquity, 82
I moralize two meanings in one word. 83

PRINCE EDWARD

That Julius Caesar was a famous man :
With what his valor did enrich his wit, 85
His wit set down to make his valor live.
Death makes no conquest of this conqueror,
For now he lives in fame, though not in life.
I'll tell you what, my cousin Buckingham –

BUCKINGHAM

What, my gracious lord ?

PRINCE EDWARD

An if I live until I be a man, 91
I'll win our ancient right in France again
Or die a soldier as I lived a king.

RICHARD *[aside]*

Short summers lightly have a forward spring. 94
      *Enter [the] young [Duke of] York, Hastings, and
      Cardinal [Bourchier].*

BUCKINGHAM

Now in good time, here comes the Duke of York.

PRINCE EDWARD

Richard of York, how fares our loving brother ?

YORK

Well, my dread lord – so must I call you now. 97

PRINCE EDWARD

Ay, brother – to our grief, as it is yours :

---

81 *characters* written records   82 *formal Vice, Iniquity* i.e. the conventional
Vice figure called Iniquity (the Vice in sixteenth-century morality plays
symbolized in one character all the vices)   83 *moralize . . . word* play on a
double meaning (as the Vice did) in a single phrase (i.e. *live long*, l. 79)   85
what that with which   91 *An if* if   94 *Short . . . spring* i.e. those who die
young are usually (*lightly*) precocious (proverbial; cf. l. 79)   97 *dread* to be
feared (as king)

99   Too late he died that might have kept that title,
      Which by his death hath lost much majesty.

RICHARD
      How fares our cousin, noble Lord of York?

YORK
      I thank you, gentle uncle. O, my lord,
      You said that idle weeds are fast in growth:
      The prince my brother hath outgrown me far.

RICHARD
      He hath, my lord.

YORK   And therefore is he idle?

RICHARD
      O my fair cousin, I must not say so.

YORK
107   Then he is more beholding to you than I.

RICHARD
      He may command me as my sovereign,
      But you have power in me as in a kinsman.

YORK
      I pray you, uncle, give me this dagger.

RICHARD
111   My dagger, little cousin? With all my heart.

PRINCE EDWARD
      A beggar, brother?

YORK
      Of my kind uncle, that I know will give,
      And being but a toy, which is no grief to give.

RICHARD
      A greater gift than that I'll give my cousin.

YORK
      A greater gift? O, that's the sword to it.

RICHARD
      Ay, gentle cousin, were it light enough.

99 *late* recently   107 *beholding* indebted   111 *My . . . heart* (Richard would,
with all his heart, like to give York his dagger in his heart)

YORK
    O, then I see you will part but with light gifts !   118
    In weightier things you'll say a beggar nay.

RICHARD
    It is too heavy for your grace to wear.

YORK
    I weigh it lightly, wcre it heavier.   121

RICHARD
    What, would you have my weapon, little lord ?

YORK
    I would, that I might thank you as you call me.

RICHARD How ?

YORK Little.

PRINCE EDWARD
    My Lord of York will still be cross in talk.
    Uncle, your grace knows how to bear with him.   126

YORK
    You mean, to bear me, not to bear with me.
    Uncle, my brother mocks both you and me :
    Because that I am little, like an ape,
    He thinks that you should bear me on your shoulders.

BUCKINGHAM [aside to Hastings]
    With what a sharp-provided wit he reasons !   132
    To mitigate the scorn he gives his uncle,
    He prettily and aptly taunts himself :
    So cunning, and so young, is wonderful.

RICHARD
    My lord, will't please you pass along ?
    Myself and my good cousin Buckingham
    Will to your mother, to entreat of her
    To meet you at the Tower and welcome you.

YORK
    What, will you go unto the Tower, my lord ?

---

118 *light* slight or trivial   121 *weigh it lightly* consider it of little value   126 *still be cross* i.e. always be twisting words   132 *sharp-provided* keenly thought out

PRINCE EDWARD
My Lord Protector needs will have it so.

YORK
I shall not sleep in quiet at the Tower.

RICHARD
Why, what should you fear?

YORK
Marry, my uncle Clarence' angry ghost:
My grandam told me he was murd'red there.

PRINCE EDWARD
I fear no uncles dead.

RICHARD
Nor none that live, I hope.

PRINCE EDWARD
148   An if they live, I hope I need not fear.
But come, my lord; with a heavy heart,
Thinking on them, go I unto the Tower.
*A sennet. Exeunt Prince [Edward], York, Hastings
[, Cardinal Bourchier, and others]. Manent Richard,
Buckingham, and Catesby.*

BUCKINGHAM
151   Think you, my lord, this little prating York
152   Was not incensèd by his subtle mother
To taunt and scorn you thus opprobriously?

RICHARD
154   No doubt, no doubt. O, 'tis a perilous boy,
Bold, quick, ingenious, forward, capable:
156   He is all the mother's, from the top to toe.

BUCKINGHAM
157   Well, let them rest. Come hither, Catesby.
Thou art sworn as deeply to effect what we intend

148 *they* i.e. Rivers and Grey (Grey was actually Prince Edward's step-brother) 151 *prating* overtalkative 152 *incensèd* incited 154 *perilous* shrewd or dangerously cunning (cf. *parlous*, II, iv, 35, the more usual form, but Richard's use of the stronger form may here be intentional) 156 *He . . . mother's* i.e. he takes after his mother 157 *let them rest* i.e. leave them (for the moment)

As closely to conceal what we impart.
Thou know'st our reasons urged upon the way.
What think'st thou? Is it not an easy matter
To make William Lord Hastings of our mind
For the instalment of this noble duke 163
In the seat royal of this famous isle?

CATESBY
He for his father's sake so loves the prince
That he will not be won to aught against him.

BUCKINGHAM
What think'st thou then of Stanley? Will not he? 167

CATESBY
He will do all in all as Hastings doth.

BUCKINGHAM
Well then, no more but this: go, gentle Catesby,
And, as it were far off, sound thou Lord Hastings
How he doth stand affected to our purpose, 171
And summon him to-morrow to the Tower
To sit about the coronation. 173
If thou dost find him tractable to us, 174
Encourage him, and tell him all our reasons:
If he be leaden, icy, cold, unwilling,
Be thou so too, and so break off the talk,
And give us notice of his inclination;
For we to-morrow hold divided councils, 179
Wherein thyself shalt highly be employed.

RICHARD
Commend me to Lord William. Tell him, Catesby, 181
His ancient knot of dangerous adversaries
To-morrow are let blood at Pomfret Castle,
And bid my lord, for joy of this good news,
Give Mistress Shore one gentle kiss the more.

---

163 *instalment* formal installation   167 *Stanley* i.e. the Earl of Derby, Lord
Stanley   171 *How . . . affected* how he is disposed   173 *sit* i.e. hold consultation   174 *tractable* compliant   179 *divided councils* i.e. two separate
council meetings (cf. III, ii, 12–14), one a private consultation unknown to
the public council   181 *Lord William* i.e. Hastings

BUCKINGHAM
  Good Catesby, go effect this business soundly.
CATESBY
  My good lords both, with all the heed I can.
RICHARD
  Shall we hear from you, Catesby, ere we sleep?
CATESBY
  You shall, my lord.
RICHARD
  At Crosby House, there shall you find us both.
                                          Exit Catesby.

BUCKINGHAM
  Now, my lord, what shall we do if we perceive
192 Lord Hastings will not yield to our complots?
RICHARD
  Chop off his head! Something we will determine.
194 And look when I am king, claim thou of me
195 The earldom of Hereford and all the moveables
     Whereof the king my brother was possessed.
BUCKINGHAM
  I'll claim that promise at your grace's hand.
RICHARD
  And look to have it yielded with all kindness.
199 Come, let us sup betimes, that afterwards
     We may digest our complots in some form.   *Exeunt.*

*

III, ii   *Enter a Messenger to the door of Hastings.*
MESSENGER
  My lord! my lord!
HASTINGS *[within]*
  Who knocks?

192 *complots* conspiracies 194 *look when* as soon as 195 *moveables* (cf.
Holinshed: 'a great quantitie of the kings treasure, and of his household
stuffe') 199 *betimes* soon
III, ii Before Lord Hastings' house

MESSENGER
One from the Lord Stanley.
Enter Lord Hastings.

HASTINGS
What is't a clock?

MESSENGER
Upon the stroke of four.

HASTINGS
Cannot my Lord Stanley sleep these tedious nights? 6

MESSENGER
So it appears by that I have to say:
First, he commends him to your noble self.

HASTINGS
What then?

MESSENGER
Then certifies your lordship that this night
He dreamt the boar had rasèd off his helm: 11
Besides, he says there are two councils kept;
And that may be determined at the one
Which may make you and him to rue at th' other. 14
Therefore he sends to know your lordship's pleasure,
If you will presently take horse with him 16
And with all speed post with him toward the North
To shun the danger that his soul divines.

HASTINGS
Go, fellow, go, return unto thy lord;
Bid him not fear the separated council.
His honor and myself are at the one,
And at the other is my good friend Catesby;
Where nothing can proceed that toucheth us
Whereof I shall not have intelligence.
Tell him his fears are shallow, without instance; 25

---

6 *tedious* (this word seems to suggest that Hastings cannot sleep either) 11
boar (see I, iii, 227); *rasèd . . . helm* figuratively, cut off his head 14 *rue*
grieve (at what was decided) 16 *presently* at once 25 *instance* evidence

And for his dreams, I wonder he's so simple
To trust the mock'ry of unquiet slumbers.
To fly the boar before the boar pursues
Were to incense the boar to follow us,
And make pursuit where he did mean no chase.
Go, bid thy master rise and come to me,
And we will both together to the Tower,
Where he shall see the boar will use us kindly.

MESSENGER
    I'll go, my lord, and tell him what you say.   *Exit.*
        Enter Catesby.

CATESBY
    Many good morrows to my noble lord!

HASTINGS
    Good morrow, Catesby; you are early stirring.
    What news, what news, in this our tott'ring state?

CATESBY
38 It is a reeling world indeed, my lord,
    And, I believe will never stand upright
    Till Richard wear the garland of the realm.

HASTINGS
    How! wear the garland! Dost thou mean the crown?

CATESBY
    Ay, my good lord.

HASTINGS
43 I'll have this crown of mine cut from my shoulders
    Before I'll see the crown so foul misplaced.
    But canst thou guess that he doth aim at it?

CATESBY
46 Ay, on my life, and hopes to find you forward
    Upon his party for the gain thereof;
    And thereupon he sends you this good news,
    That this same very day your enemies,
    The kindred of the queen, must die at Pomfret.

---

38 *reeling* (cf. II, iii, 5)   43 *crown . . . shoulders* (foreshadows Hastings' death
and looks back to l. 11)   46–47 *forward Upon* lending strong support to

HASTINGS

    Indeed I am no mourner for that news,

    Because they have been still my adversaries;

    But that I'll give my voice on Richard's side   52

    To bar my master's heirs in true descent –

    God knows I will not do it, to the death!

CATESBY

    God keep your lordship in that gracious mind!

HASTINGS

    But I shall laugh at this a twelvemonth hence,   57

    That they which brought me in my master's hate,

    I live to look upon their tragedy.

    Well, Catesby, ere a fortnight make me older,

    I'll send some packing that yet think not on't.

CATESBY

    'Tis a vile thing to die, my gracious lord,

    When men are unprepared and look not for it.

HASTINGS

    O monstrous, monstrous! and so falls it out

    With Rivers, Vaughan, Grey; and so 'twill do

    With some men else, that think themselves as safe

    As thou and I, who (as thou know'st) are dear

    To princely Richard and to Buckingham.

CATESBY

    The princes both make high account of you –

        [Aside]

    For they account his head upon the Bridge.   70

HASTINGS

    I know they do, and I have well deserved it.

        Enter Lord Stanley [Earl of Derby].

    Come on, come on! Where is your boar-spear, man?

    Fear you the boar, and go so unprovided?

DERBY

    My lord, good morrow. Good morrow, Catesby.

---

52 *still* always   57–59 *But . . . tragedy* (construction difficult; for the sense,
omit *they* in l. 58 and insert l. 59 after *That* in l. 58)   70 *Bridge* London
Bridge (traitors' heads were displayed on poles on its gateway entrances)

75   You may jest on, but, by the Holy Rood,
I do not like these several councils, I.

HASTINGS
My lord,
I hold my life as dear as you do yours,
And never in my days, I do protest,
Was it so precious to me as 'tis now.
Think you, but that I know our state secure,
82   I would be so triumphant as I am?

DERBY
The lords at Pomfret, when they rode from London,
84   Were jocund and supposed their states were sure,
And they indeed had no cause to mistrust;
But yet you see how soon the day o'ercast.
87   This sudden stab of rancor I misdoubt:
Pray God, I say, I prove a needless coward!
89   What, shall we toward the Tower? The day is spent.

HASTINGS
Come, come, have with you. Wot you what, my lord?
To-day the lords you talked of are beheaded.

DERBY
They, for their truth, might better wear their heads
93   Than some that have accused them wear their hats.
94   But come, my lord, let's away.
Enter a Pursuivant [also named Hastings].

HASTINGS
Go on before. I'll talk with this good fellow.
*Exeunt Lord Stanley [Earl of Derby],
and Catesby.*

---

75 *Holy Rood* Christ's cross   **82** *triumphant* exultant   **84** *jocund* merry   **87** *This . . . misdoubt* i.e. I fear this sudden blow (the capture of Rivers, Vaughan, and Grey) arising out of hatred   **89** *day is spent* (the folio reading is questionable since it is just after 4 a.m.; the quartos omit the time reference)   **93** *some . . . hats* (probably a veiled reference to Richard and Buckingham, whose rank as dukes gave them the privilege of wearing the so-called ducal cap in the royal presence, no head-covering resembling a hat being allowed below the rank of duke)   **94 s.d.** *Pursuivant* state messenger with authority to execute warrants

How now, sirrah? How goes the world with thee?

PURSUIVANT
The better that your lordship please to ask.

HASTINGS
I tell thee, man, 'tis better with me now
Than when thou met'st me last where now we meet.
Then was I going prisoner to the Tower
By the suggestion of the queen's allies;
But now I tell thee (keep it to thyself)
This day those enemies are put to death,
And I in better state than e'er I was.

PURSUIVANT
God hold it, to your honor's good content!   105

HASTINGS
Gramercy, fellow. There, drink that for me.   106
    Throws him his purse.

PURSUIVANT I thank your honor.   *Exit Pursuivant.*
    Enter a Priest.

PRIEST
Well met, my lord. I am glad to see your honor.

HASTINGS
I thank thee, good Sir John, with all my heart.   109
I am in your debt for your last exercise;   110
Come the next Sabbath, and I will content you.
    [He whispers in his ear.]

PRIEST
I'll wait upon your lordship.
    Enter Buckingham.

BUCKINGHAM
What, talking with a priest, Lord Chamberlain?
Your friends at Pomfret, they do need the priest;
Your honor hath no shriving work in hand.   115

---

105 *God hold it* i.e. may God continue this state of affairs   106 *Gramercy*
much thanks   109 *Sir John* ('sir' was a title of respect applied to the clergy;
no reference here to knighthood)   110 *exercise* sermon   115 *shriving work*
i.e. 'deathbed' confessions

HASTINGS
    Good faith, and when I met this holy man,
    The men you talk of came into my mind.
    What, go you toward the Tower?
BUCKINGHAM
    I do, my lord, but long I cannot stay there.
    I shall return before your lordship thence.
HASTINGS
    Nay, like enough, for I stay dinner there.
BUCKINGHAM [aside]
    And supper too, although thou know'st it not. –
    Come, will you go?
HASTINGS   I'll wait upon your lordship. Exeunt.

*

III, iii   Enter Sir Richard Ratcliffe, with Halberds, carrying
               the Nobles [Rivers, Grey, and Vaughan] to death at
               Pomfret.
[RATCLIFFE Come, bring forth the prisoners.]
RIVERS
    Sir Richard Ratcliffe, let me tell thee this:
    To-day shalt thou behold a subject die
    For truth, for duty, and for loyalty.
GREY
    God bless the prince from all the pack of you!
    A knot you are of damnèd bloodsuckers.
VAUGHAN
    You live that shall cry woe for this hereafter.
RATCLIFFE
    Dispatch! The limit of your lives is out.
RIVERS
    O Pomfret, Pomfret! O thou bloody prison,
    Fatal and ominous to noble peers!

III, iii Pomfret Castle

Within the guilty closure of thy walls
Richard the Second here was hacked to death ;
And, for more slander to thy dismal seat,   13
We give to thee our guiltless blood to drink.

GREY

Now Margaret's curse is fall'n upon our heads,
When she exclaimed on Hastings, you, and I,
For standing by when Richard stabbed her son.

RIVERS

Then cursed she Richard, then cursed she Buckingham,
Then cursed she Hastings. O, remember, God,
To hear her prayer for them, as now for us !
And for my sister and her princely sons,
Be satisfied, dear God, with our true blood,
Which, as thou know'st, unjustly must be spilt.

RATCLIFFE

Make haste. The hour of death is expiate.   24

RIVERS

Come, Grey ; come, Vaughan ; let us here embrace.
Farewell, until we meet again in heaven.   *Exeunt.*

*

Enter Buckingham, [Lord Stanley Earl of] Derby,   III, iv
Hastings, Bishop of Ely, Norfolk, Ratcliffe, Lovel,
with others, at a table.

HASTINGS

Now, noble peers, the cause why we are met
Is to determine of the coronation.   2
In God's name, speak. When is the royal day ?

BUCKINGHAM

Is all things ready for the royal time ?

13 *for . . . seat* i.e. in order to bring greater shame upon Pomfret, a place
which already bodes disaster   24 *expiate* fully come (cf. l. 8)
III, iv Within the Tower of London   2 *determine of* come to a decision
concerning

DERBY
5   It is, and wants but nomination.

BISHOP OF ELY
To-morrow then I judge a happy day.

BUCKINGHAM
Who knows the Lord Protector's mind herein?
8   Who is most inward with the noble duke?

BISHOP OF ELY
Your grace, we think, should soonest know his mind.

BUCKINGHAM
We know each other's faces; for our hearts,
He knows no more of mine than I of yours;
Or I of his, my lord, than you of mine.
Lord Hastings, you and he are near in love.

HASTINGS
I thank his grace, I know he loves me well;
But, for his purpose in the coronation,
16   I have not sounded him, nor he delivered
His gracious pleasure any way therein;
But you, my honorable lords, may name the time,
And in the duke's behalf I'll give my voice,
Which, I presume, he'll take in gentle part.
        Enter [Richard, Duke of] Gloucester.

BISHOP OF ELY
In happy time, here comes the duke himself.

RICHARD
My noble lords and cousins all, good morrow.
I have been long a sleeper; but I trust
24   My absence doth neglect no great design
Which by my presence might have been concluded.

BUCKINGHAM
Had you not come upon your cue, my lord,
William Lord Hastings had pronounced your part—
I mean, your voice for crowning of the king.

5 *nomination* the fixing   8 *inward* intimate   16 *I . . . him* (but Richard had in fact sounded Hastings; cf. l. 36)   24 *neglect . . . design* i.e. cause no great design to be neglected

RICHARD

Than my Lord Hastings no man might be bolder.
His lordship knows me well, and loves me well.
My Lord of Ely, when I was last in Holborn
I saw good strawberries in your garden there.
I do beseech you send for some of them.

BISHOP OF ELY

Marry and will, my lord, with all my heart. *Exit Bishop.*

RICHARD

Cousin of Buckingham, a word with you.
    [Takes him aside.]
Catesby hath sounded Hastings in our business
And finds the testy gentleman so hot   37
That he will lose his head ere give consent
His master's child, as worshipfully he terms it,   39
Shall lose the royalty of England's throne.   40

BUCKINGHAM

Withdraw yourself awhile. I'll go with you.
                    Exeunt [Richard and Buckingham].

DERBY

We have not yet set down this day of triumph:
To-morrow, in my judgment, is too sudden;
For I myself am not so well provided
As else I would be, were the day prolonged.   45
    Enter the Bishop of Ely.

BISHOP OF ELY

Where is my lord the Duke of Gloucester?
I have sent for these strawberries.

HASTINGS

His grace looks cheerfully and smooth this morning;
There's some conceit or other likes him well   49
When that he bids good morrow with such spirit.
I think there's never a man in Christendom
Can lesser hide his love or hate than he,

---

37 *testy* quick-tempered; *hot* burning (with his resolve)   39 *worshipfully* i.e.
using words expressing honor or regard   40 *royalty* sovereignty   45 *the
day prolonged* i.e. a later day set   49 *conceit* (happy) idea or device

For by his face straight shall you know his heart.

DERBY

What of his heart perceive you in his face
55 By any livelihood he showed to-day?

HASTINGS

Marry, that with no man here he is offended;
For were he, he had shown it in his looks.

[DERBY

I pray God he be not, I say.]
Enter Richard and Buckingham.

RICHARD

I pray you all, tell me what they deserve
That do conspire my death with devilish plots
61 Of damnèd witchcraft, and that have prevailed
Upon my body with their hellish charms.

HASTINGS

The tender love I bear your grace, my lord,
Makes me most forward in this princely presence
To doom th' offenders, whosoe'er they be:
I say, my lord, they have deservèd death.

RICHARD

Then be your eyes the witness of their evil.
Look how I am bewitched. Behold, mine arm
Is like a blasted sapling, withered up;
And this is Edward's wife, that monstrous witch,
71 Consorted with that harlot, strumpet Shore,
That by their witchcraft thus have markèd me.

HASTINGS

If they have done this deed, my noble lord—

RICHARD

If? Thou protector of this damnèd strumpet,
Talk'st thou to me of ifs? Thou art a traitor.
Off with his head! Now by Saint Paul I swear
I will not dine until I see the same.

55 *livelihood* vivacity   61–62 *prevailed Upon* got the better of   71 *Consorted* associated

Lovel and Ratcliffe, look that it be done:
The rest that love me, rise and follow me.
                        Exeunt. Manent Lovel and Ratcliffe,
                                    with the Lord Hastings.

HASTINGS
  Woe, woe for England, not a whit for me!   80
  For I, too fond, might have prevented this.   81
  Stanley did dream the boar did rase our helms;
  But I did scorn it and disdain to fly.
  Three times to-day my footcloth horse did stumble,   84
  And started when he looked upon the Tower,
  As loath to bear me to the slaughterhouse.
  O, now I need the priest that spake to me!
  I now repent I told the pursuivant,
  As too triumphing, how mine enemies   89
  To-day at Pomfret bloodily were butchered,
  And I myself secure, in grace and favor.   91
  O Margaret, Margaret, now thy heavy curse
  Is lighted on poor Hastings' wretched head!

RATCLIFFE
  Come, come, dispatch! The duke would be at dinner.
  Make a short shrift; he longs to see your head.

HASTINGS
  O momentary grace of mortal men,   96
  Which we more hunt for than the grace of God!
  Who builds his hope in air of your good looks   98
  Lives like a drunken sailor on a mast,
  Ready with every nod to tumble down
  Into the fatal bowels of the deep.

LOVEL
  Come, come, dispatch! 'Tis bootless to exclaim.   102

HASTINGS
  O bloody Richard! Miserable England!

---

80 *whit* bit 81 *fond* foolish 84 *footcloth horse* horse caparisoned with a
richly wrought covering reaching almost to the ground 89 *triumphing*
exulting 91 *secure* (1) safe, (2) careless 96 *grace* favor 98 *of . . . looks* out
of your kind glances (suggesting approval) 102 *bootless* useless

I prophesy the fearfull'st time to thee
That ever wretched age hath looked upon.
Come, lead me to the block ; bear him my head.
They smile at me who shortly shall be dead.   *Exeunt.*

*

III, v   *Enter Richard [Duke of Gloucester], and*
              Buckingham, in rotten armor, marvellous ill-favored.

RICHARD
Come, cousin, canst thou quake and change thy color,
Murder thy breath in middle of a word,
And then again begin, and stop again,
As if thou were distraught and mad with terror ?

BUCKINGHAM
Tut, I can counterfeit the deep tragedian,
Speak and look back, and pry on every side,
Tremble and start at wagging of a straw :
8   Intending deep suspicion, ghastly looks
       Are at my service, like enforcèd smiles ;
10   And both are ready in their offices,
       At any time to grace my stratagems.
       But what, is Catesby gone ?

RICHARD
He is ; and see, he brings the Mayor along.
              Enter the Mayor and Catesby.

BUCKINGHAM
Lord Mayor –

RICHARD
Look to the drawbridge there !

BUCKINGHAM
Hark ! a drum.

RICHARD
17   Catesby, o'erlook the walls.

III, v The walls of the Tower   s.d. *rotten* rusty ; *ill-favored* ugly   8 *Intending* pretending   10 *offices* particular functions   17 *o'erlook* inspect

BUCKINGHAM

Lord Mayor, the reason we have sent –

RICHARD

Look back! defend thee! Here are enemies!

BUCKINGHAM

God and our innocence defend and guard us!

Enter Lovel and Ratcliffe, with Hastings' head.

RICHARD

Be patient, they are friends – Ratcliffe and Lovel.

LOVEL

Here is the head of that ignoble traitor,
The dangerous and unsuspected Hastings.

RICHARD

So dear I loved the man that I must weep:
I took him for the plainest harmless creature
That breathed upon the earth a Christian;   25
Made him my book, wherein my soul recorded   27
The history of all her secret thoughts.
So smooth he daubed his vice with show of virtue
That, his apparent open guilt omitted –
I mean, his conversation with Shore's wife –   31
He lived from all attainder of suspects.   32

BUCKINGHAM

Well, well, he was the covert'st shelt'red traitor   33
That ever lived. [Look ye, my Lord Mayor.]
Would you imagine, or almost believe,
Were't not that by great preservation   36
We live to tell it, that the subtle traitor
This day had plotted, in the Council House,
To murder me and my good Lord of Gloucester?

MAYOR

Had he done so?

25 *harmless* (supply 'most'; cf. l. 33)   27 *book* i.e. table book or 'diary'
31 *conversation* sexual intimacy   32 *attainder of suspects* stain of suspicions
33 *shelt'red* hidden (supply 'most')   36 *great preservation* i.e. the fortunate
forestalling of an evil that might have happened

RICHARD

What? Think you we are Turks or infidels?
Or that we would, against the form of law,
Proceed thus rashly in the villain's death
But that the extreme peril of the case,
The peace of England, and our persons' safety
Enforced us to this execution?

MAYOR

Now fair befall you! He deserved his death,
48   And your good graces both have well proceeded
To warn false traitors from the like attempts.

BUCKINGHAM

I never looked for better at his hands
After he once fell in with Mistress Shore:
Yet had we not determined he should die
Until your lordship came to see his end,
Which now the loving haste of these our friends,
55   Something against our meanings, have prevented;
Because, my lord, I would have had you heard
57   The traitor speak, and timorously confess
The manner and the purpose of his treasons,
That you might well have signified the same
60   Unto the citizens, who haply may
61   Misconster us in him and wail his death.

MAYOR

But, my good lord, your grace's words shall serve,
As well as I had seen, and heard him speak;
And do not doubt, right noble princes both,
But I'll acquaint our duteous citizens
66   With all your just proceedings in this cause.

RICHARD

And to that end we wished your lordship here,
68   T' avoid the censures of the carping world.

---

48 *proceeded* done   55 *prevented* anticipated   57 *timorously* full of fear   60 *haply* perhaps   61 *Misconster . . . him* i.e. misunderstand our manner of dealing with him   66 *cause* affair or action (perhaps with legal overtones)   68 *carping* overcritical

BUCKINGHAM

But since you come too late of our intent,   69
Yet witness what you hear we did intend: 70
And so, my good Lord Mayor, we bid farewell.

Exit Mayor.

RICHARD

Go after, after, cousin Buckingham.
The Mayor towards Guildhall hies him in all post: 73
There, at your meet'st advantage of the time,   74
Infer the bastardy of Edward's children.
Tell them how Edward put to death a citizen
Only for saying he would make his son
Heir to the Crown, meaning indeed his house,   78
Which by the sign thereof was termèd so.
Moreover, urge his hateful luxury   80
And bestial appetite in change of lust,   81
Which stretched unto their servants, daughters, wives,
Even where his raging eye or savage heart,
Without control, lusted to make a prey.
Nay, for a need, thus far come near my person:
Tell them, when that my mother went with child
Of that insatiate Edward, noble York,
My princely father, then had wars in France,
And by true computation of the time
Found that the issue was not his begot;
Which well appearèd in his lineaments,
Being nothing like the noble duke my father.
Yet touch this sparingly, as 'twere far off,
Because, my lord, you know my mother lives.

BUCKINGHAM

Doubt not, my lord, I'll play the orator
As if the golden fee for which I plead   96

---

69 *of* i.e. in terms of   70 *witness* i.e. bear witness to   73 *Guildhall* the 'town hall' of London; *post* haste   74 *meet'st . . . time* i.e. the psychological moment   78 *Crown . . . house* i.e. a tavern called 'The Crown'   80 *luxury* lasciviousness   81 *change of lust* i.e. alteration in the object of his lust   96 *golden fee* i.e. the crown (play on 'lawyer's fee')

Were for myself – and so, my lord, adieu.

RICHARD

98   If you thrive well, bring them to Baynard's Castle,
Where you shall find me well accompanied
With reverend fathers and well-learnèd bishops.

BUCKINGHAM

I go ; and towards three or four a clock
Look for the news that the Guildhall affords.
Exit Buckingham.

RICHARD

103 Go, Lovel, with all speed to Doctor Shaw –
[*To Catesby*]
104 Go thou to Friar Penker. – Bid them both
Meet me within this hour at Baynard's Castle.
Exeunt [Lovel, Catesby, and Ratcliffe].
106 Now will I go to take some privy order
To draw the brats of Clarence out of sight,
108 And to give order that no manner person
Have any time recourse unto the princes.   *Exit.*

*

III, vi   *Enter a Scrivener [with a paper in his hand].*

SCRIVENER

Here is the indictment of the good Lord Hastings,
2   Which in a set hand fairly is engrossed
3   That it may be to-day read o'er in Paul's.
And mark how well the sequel hangs together :
Eleven hours I have spent to write it over,
For yesternight by Catesby was it sent me ;

98 *Baynard's Castle* Richard's stronghold between Blackfriars and London
Bridge   103, 104 *Shaw, Penker* well-known preachers   106 *take . . . order*
make some secret arrangement   108–09 *no . . . unto* i.e. no person of any sort
should have, at any time, admittance to
III, vi Before Baynard's Castle   2 *in . . . engrossed* is written neatly in a
formal legal hand   3 *Paul's* i.e. St Paul's Cathedral

The handwritten margin notes: "the writer is in control – Shakespeare tells us the writer is in control –"

The precedent was full as long a-doing;   7
And yet within these five hours Hastings lived,
Untainted, unexamined, free, at liberty.
Here's a good world the while! Who is so gross   10
That cannot see this palpable device?
Yet who's so bold but says he sees it not?
Bad is the world, and all will come to nought
When such ill dealing must be seen in thought.   14

Margin note: "people don't tell what's going on"

                                                    Exit.

Enter Richard [Duke of Gloucester] and   III, vii
Buckingham at several doors.

RICHARD
How now, how now? What say the citizens?

BUCKINGHAM
Now, by the holy Mother of our Lord,
The citizens are mum, say not a word.

RICHARD
Touched you the bastardy of Edward's children?

BUCKINGHAM
I did, with his contract with Lady Lucy   5
And his contract by deputy in France;   6
Th' unsatiate greediness of his desire
And his enforcement of the city wives;
His tyranny for trifles; his own bastardy,
As being got, your father then in France,
And his resemblance, being not like the duke.
Withal I did infer your lineaments,
Being the right idea of your father   13
Both in your form and nobleness of mind;
Laid open all your victories in Scotland,

---

7 *precedent* exemplar (i.e. the prepared indictment)   **10** *the while* just now;
gross stupid   **14** *seen in thought* expressed only in thinking
III, vii   **5** *Lady Lucy* Elizabeth Lucy (to whom Edward IV was not actually
contracted, although she bore him a child)   **6** *contract . . . France* (reference
to Edward IV's overtures for marriage with Bona, sister-in-law of Lewis IX
of France; cf. *3 Henry VI*, III, iii, and below, ll. 181–82)   **13** *right idea* true
image

Your discipline in war, wisdom in peace,
Your bounty, virtue, fair humility ;
Indeed, left nothing fitting for your purpose
Untouched, or slightly handlèd in discourse ;
And when mine oratory drew to an end,
I bid them that did love their country's good
Cry, 'God save Richard, England's royal king !'

RICHARD
And did they so ?

BUCKINGHAM
No, so God help me, they spake not a word,
But, like dumb statuës or breathing stones,
Stared each on other, and looked deadly pale.
Which when I saw, I reprehended them
And asked the Mayor what meant this wilful silence.
His answer was, the people were not usèd
30   To be spoke to but by the Recorder.
Then he was urged to tell my tale again :
'Thus saith the duke, thus hath the duke inferred,'—
But nothing spake in warrant from himself.
When he had done, some followers of mine own,
At lower end of the hall, hurled up their caps,
And some ten voices cried, 'God save King Richard !'
And thus I took the vantage of those few :
'Thanks, gentle citizens and friends,' quoth I.
'This general applause and cheerful shout
Argues your wisdoms and your love to Richard'—
And even here brake off and came away.

RICHARD
What tongueless blocks were they ! Would they not
      speak ?

[BUCKINGHAM
No, by my troth, my lord.]

30 *Recorder* (a magistrate appointed by the mayor and aldermen to serve as an 'oral record' of proceedings in city law courts and government)

RICHARD

    Will not the Mayor then and his brethren come?

BUCKINGHAM

    The Mayor is here at hand. Intend some fear;   45
    Be not you spoke with but by mighty suit;   46
    And look you get a prayer book in your hand
    And stand between two churchmen, good my lord,
    For on that ground I'll make a holy descant;   49
    And be not easily won to our requests.
    Play the maid's part: still answer nay, and take it.   51

RICHARD

    I go; and if you plead as well for them
    As I can say nay to thee for myself,
    No doubt we bring it to a happy issue.

BUCKINGHAM

    Go, go, up to the leads! The Lord Mayor knocks.   55
                    [Exit Richard.]
     Enter the Mayor [, Aldermen,] and Citizens.
    Welcome, my lord. I dance attendance here;
    I think the duke will not be spoke withal.   57
     Enter Catesby.
    Now, Catesby, what says your lord to my request?

CATESBY

    He doth entreat your grace, my noble lord,
    To visit him to-morrow or next day:
    He is within, with two right reverend fathers,
    Divinely bent to meditation,   62
    And in no worldly suits would he be moved
    To draw him from his holy exercise.

BUCKINGHAM

    Return, good Catesby, to the gracious duke:
    Tell him, myself, the Mayor and Aldermen,

---

45 *Intend* pretend   46 *by mighty suit* by great solicitation   49 *descant* (see I, i, 27)   51 *maid's* girl's; *answer . . . it* i.e. keep saying no, but at the same time accept whatever is being offered (proverbial)   55 *leads* sheets of metal used to cover a (flat) roof   57 *withal* with   62 *Divinely bent* (1) spiritually inclined, (2) kneeling like a divine (cf. l. 73)

In deep designs, in matter of great moment,
68   No less importing than our general good,
Are come to have some conference with his grace.

CATESBY
I'll signify so much unto him straight.   *Exit.*

BUCKINGHAM
Ah ha, my lord! this prince is not an Edward.
72   He is not lulling on a lewd love-bed,
But on his knees at meditation;
Not dallying with a brace of courtesans,
75   But meditating with two deep divines;
76   Not sleeping, to engross his idle body,
But praying, to enrich his watchful soul.
Happy were England, would this virtuous prince
Take on his grace the sovereignty thereof;
But sure I fear we shall not win him to it.

MAYOR
81   Marry, God defend his grace should say us nay!

BUCKINGHAM
I fear he will. Here Catesby comes again.
      Enter Catesby.
Now, Catesby, what says his grace?

CATESBY   My lord,
He wonders to what end you have assembl èd
Such troops of citizens to come to him,
His grace not being warned thereof before:
He fears, my lord, you mean no good to him.

BUCKINGHAM
Sorry I am my noble cousin should
Suspect me that I mean no good to him:
90   By heaven, we come to him in perfit love;
And so once more return and tell his grace.
                              Exit [Catesby].

68 *No . . . than* i.e. of no less significance than one concerned with   72
lulling lolling, lounging   75 *deep* i.e. spiritually and academically learned
76 *engross* fatten   81 *defend* forbid   90 *perfit* perfect

When holy and devout religious men
Are at their beads, 'tis much to draw them thence,   93
So sweet is zealous contemplation.
    *Enter Richard aloft, between two Bishops. [Catesby
    returns.]*

MAYOR
See where his grace stands, 'tween two clergymen.

BUCKINGHAM
Two props of virtue for a Christian prince,
To stay him from the fall of vanity;   97
And see, a book of prayer in his hand —
True ornaments to know a holy man.   99
Famous Plantagenet, most gracious prince,
Lend favorable ear to our requests,
And pardon us the interruption
Of thy devotion and right Christian zeal.

RICHARD
My lord, there needs no such apology:
I do beseech your grace to pardon me,
Who, earnest in the service of my God,
Deferred the visitation of my friends.
But, leaving this, what is your grace's pleasure?

BUCKINGHAM
Even that (I hope) which pleaseth God above
And all good men of this ungoverned isle.

RICHARD
I do suspect I have done some offense
That seems disgracious in the city's eye,   112
And that you come to reprehend my ignorance.

BUCKINGHAM
You have, my lord. Would it might please your grace,
On our entreaties, to amend your fault!

RICHARD
Else wherefore breathe I in a Christian land?

93 *'tis much* i.e. it takes a great deal 97 *fall of vanity* downfall caused by
vanity 99 *ornaments* (referring to the clergymen and prayer book) 112
disgracious-disliked

BUCKINGHAM

 Know then it is your fault that you resign
 The supreme seat, the throne majestical,
 The scept'red office of your ancestors,
120 Your state of fortune and your due of birth,
 The lineal glory of your royal house,
 To the corruption of a blemished stock;
123 Whiles, in the mildness of your sleepy thoughts,
 Which here we waken to our country's good,
125 The noble isle doth want her proper limbs;
 Her face defaced with scars of infamy,
 Her royal stock graft with ignoble plants,
128 And almost should'red in the swallowing gulf
 Of dark forgetfulness and deep oblivion.
130 Which to recure, we heartily solicit
 Your gracious self to take on you the charge
 And kingly government of this your land;
 Not as Protector, steward, substitute,
134 Or lowly factor for another's gain;
135 But as successively, from blood to blood,
136 Your right of birth, your empery, your own.
 For this, consorted with the citizens,
 Your very worshipful and loving friends,
 And by their vehement instigation,
 In this just cause come I to move your grace.

RICHARD

 I cannot tell if to depart in silence,
 Or bitterly to speak in your reproof,
143 Best fitteth my degree or your condition.
 If not to answer, you might haply think
145 Tongue-tied ambition, not replying, yielded

---

120 *state of fortune* position of greatness **123** *sleepy* reposeful **125** *proper* own **128** *should'red in* violently jostled into **130** *recure* restore to health **134** *factor* agent **135** *successively* in order of succession **136** *empery* empire or sole rule **143** *fitteth . . . condition* accords with my rank (as duke) or your social position (as commoners) **145** *Tongue-tied . . . yielded* i.e. silence yields consent (proverbial)

To bear the golden yoke of sovereignty
Which fondly you would here impose on me.   147
If to reprove you for this suit of yours,
So seasoned with your faithful love to me,   149
Then, on the other side, I checked my friends.
Therefore – to speak, and to avoid the first,
And then, in speaking, not to incur the last –
Definitively thus I answer you.   153
Your love deserves my thanks, but my desert
Unmeritable shuns your high request.
First, if all obstacles were cut away,
And that my path were even to the crown,   157
As the ripe revenue and due of birth,
Yet so much is my poverty of spirit,   159
So mighty and so many my defects,
That I would rather hide me from my greatness,
Being a bark to brook no mighty sea,   162
Than in my greatness covet to be hid   163
And in the vapor of my glory smothered.
But, God be thanked, there is no need of me,
And much I need to help you, were there need :
The royal tree hath left us royal fruit,
Which, mellowed by the stealing hours of time,
Will well become the seat of majesty
And make (no doubt) us happy by his reign.
On him I lay that you would lay on me,
The right and fortune of his happy stars,   172
Which God defend that I should wring from him !

BUCKINGHAM
My lord, this argues conscience in your grace,
But the respects thereof are nice and trivial,   175

147 *fondly* foolishly   149 *seasoned* made agreeable (given a pleasant taste)
153 *Definitively* once and for all   157 *even* without impediment   159
poverty of spirit lack of self-assertion (perhaps meant also as an indirect
compliment to himself, since 'Blessed are the poor in spirit' [Matthew v, 3])
162 *bark* small sailing vessel   163 *Than . . . hid* than desire to be enveloped
by my greatness   172 *happy* auspicious   175 *respects . . . nice* i.e. the con-
siderations on which you argue are overscrupulous

All circumstances well consider̀ed.
You say that Edward is your brother's son :
So say we too, but not by Edward's wife ;
For first was he contract to Lady Lucy –
Your mother lives a witness to his vow –
181 And afterward by substitute betrothed
To Bona, sister to the King of France.
These both put off, a poor petitioner,
A care-crazed mother to a many sons,
A beauty-waning and distress̀ed widow,
Even in the afternoon of her best days,
187 Made prize and purchase of his wanton eye,
188 Seduced the pitch and height of his degree
189 To base declension and loathed bigamy.
By her, in his unlawful bed, he got
This Edward, whom our manners call the prince.
More bitterly could I expostulate,
Save that, for reverence to some alive,
I give a sparing limit to my tongue.
195 Then, good my lord, take to your royal self
This proffered benefit of dignity ;
If not to bless us and the land withal,
Yet to draw forth your noble ancestry
From the corruption of abusing times
Unto a lineal true-deriv̀ed course.

MAYOR
Do, good my lord ; your citizens entreat you.

BUCKINGHAM
Refuse not, mighty lord, this proffered love.

CATESBY
O, make them joyful, grant their lawful suit !

RICHARD
Alas, why would you heap this care on me ?

181 *substitute* proxy   187 *purchase* booty   188 *Seduced . . . degree* i.e. led
away (or down from) the eminence and greatness associated with his noble
rank   189 *declension* falling away from a high standard   195 *good my lord*
my good lord

I am unfit for state and majesty :
I do beseech you take it not amiss,
I cannot nor I will not yield to you.

BUCKINGHAM

If you refuse it – as, in love and zeal,   208
Loath to depose the child, your brother's son ;
As well we know your tenderness of heart
And gentle, kind, effeminate remorse,   211
Which we have noted in you to your kindred
And egally indeed to all estates –   213
Yet know, whe'er you accept our suit or no,   214
Your brother's son shall never reign our king,
But we will plant some other in the throne
To the disgrace and downfall of your house ;
And in this resolution here we leave you.
Come, citizens. Zounds, I'll entreat no more !

[RICHARD

O, do not swear, my lord of Buckingham.]

> *Exeunt [Buckingham, Mayor, Aldermen,*
> *and Citizens].*

CATESBY

Call him again, sweet prince, accept their suit :
If you deny them, all the land will rue it.   222

RICHARD

Will you enforce me to a world of cares ?
Call them again. I am not made of stones,
But penetrable to your kind entreaties,
Albeit against my conscience and my soul.

> *Enter Buckingham and the rest.*

Cousin of Buckingham, and sage grave men,
Since you will buckle fortune on my back,
To bear her burden, whe'er I will or no,   229
I must have patience to endure the load ;
But if black scandal or foul-faced reproach

---

208 *as* i.e. as the result of being   211 *kind, effeminate remorse* natural, tender
pity   213 *egally* equally   214 *whe'er* whether   222 *rue* suffer for   229 *To*
i.e. in order to make me

121

232   Attend the sequel of your imposition,
233   Your mere enforcement shall acquittance me
       From all the impure blots and stains thereof;
       For God doth know, and you may partly see,
       How far I am from the desire of this.

MAYOR
God bless your grace! We see it and will say it.

RICHARD
In saying so you shall but say the truth.

BUCKINGHAM
Then I salute you with this royal title –
Long live King Richard, England's worthy king!

ALL
Amen.

BUCKINGHAM
To-morrow may it please you to be crowned?

RICHARD
Even when you please, for you will have it so.

BUCKINGHAM
To-morrow then we will attend your grace,
And so most joyfully we take our leave.

RICHARD [to the Bishops]
Come, let us to our holy work again. –
Farewell, my cousin; farewell, gentle friends.   Exeunt.

*

IV, i   Enter the Queen [Elizabeth], the Duchess of
         York, and Marquess [of] Dorset [at one door];
         Anne Duchess of Gloucester [, Lady Margaret
         Plantagenet, Clarence's young daughter, at
         another door].

DUCHESS OF YORK
Who meets us here? My niece Plantagenet,
Led in the hand of her kind aunt of Gloucester?

232 your imposition i.e. the fortune (kingship) which you lay upon me 233
mere absolute; acquittance acquit
IV, i Before the Tower

Now, for my life, she's wand'ring to the Tower   3
On pure heart's love, to greet the tender prince.
Daughter, well met.

ANNE   God give your graces both
A happy and a joyful time of day!

QUEEN ELIZABETH
As much to you, good sister. Whither away?

ANNE
No farther than the Tower, and, as I guess,
Upon the like devotion as yourselves,
To gratulate the gentle princes there.   10

QUEEN ELIZABETH
Kind sister, thanks. We'll enter all together.
          Enter the Lieutenant [Brakenbury].
And in good time, here the Lieutenant comes.
Master Lieutenant, pray you, by your leave,
How doth the prince, and my young son of York?

LIEUTENANT
Right well, dear madam. By your patience,
I may not suffer you to visit them;
The king hath strictly charged the contrary.

QUEEN ELIZABETH
The king? Who's that?

LIEUTENANT   I mean the Lord Protector.

QUEEN ELIZABETH
The Lord protect him from that kingly title!   19
Hath he set bounds between their love and me?   20
I am their mother; who shall bar me from them?

DUCHESS OF YORK
I am their father's mother; I will see them.

ANNE
Their aunt I am in law, in love their mother;
Then bring me to their sights. I'll bear thy blame

---

3 *for my life* i.e. staking my life upon it   10 *gratulate* congratulate   19 *The Lord . . . title* i.e. may God in his capacity as Richard's legal guardian exercise his authority to prevent Richard from getting the title of king   20 *bounds* barriers

25   And take thy office from thee on my peril.

LIEUTENANT

26   No, madam, no! I may not leave it so:
I am bound by oath, and therefore pardon me.

                             Exit Lieutenant.

         Enter Stanley [Earl of Derby].

DERBY

Let me but meet you, ladies, an hour hence,
And I'll salute your grace of York as mother

30   And reverend looker-on of two fair queens.
    [To Anne]
Come, madam, you must straight to Westminster,
There to be crownèd Richard's royal queen.

QUEEN ELIZABETH

33   Ah, cut my lace asunder,
That my pent heart may have some scope to beat,
Or else I swoon with this dead-killing news!

ANNE

Despiteful tidings! O unpleasing news!

DORSET

Be of good cheer. Mother, how fares your grace?

QUEEN ELIZABETH

O Dorset, speak not to me, get thee gone!
Death and destruction dogs thee at thy heels;

40   Thy mother's name is ominous to children.
If thou wilt outstrip death, go cross the seas,
And live with Richmond, from the reach of hell.
Go hie thee, hie thee from this slaughterhouse,
Lest thou increase the number of the dead
And make me die the thrall of Margaret's curse,

46   Nor mother, wife, nor England's counted queen.

DERBY

Full of wise care is this your counsel, madam:

---

25 *take . . . thee* i.e. take your office upon myself   **26** *leave it* i.e. give up my office   **30** *looker-on* beholder (or here perhaps 'guardian')   **33** *cut my lace* (Elizabethan women wore tightly laced bodices)   **40** *ominous* portending evil   **46** *counted* esteemed

Take all the swift advantage of the hours. 48
You shall have letters from me to my son 49
In your behalf, to meet you on the way : 50
Be not ta'en tardy by unwise delay. 51

DUCHESS OF YORK
O ill-dispersing wind of misery ! 52
O my accursèd womb, the bed of death !
A cockatrice hast thou hatched to the world, 54
Whose unavoided eye is murderous.

DERBY
Come, madam, come ! I in all haste was sent.

ANNE
And I with all unwillingness will go.
O, would to God that the inclusive verge 58
Of golden metal that must round my brow
Were red-hot steel, to sear me to the brains !
Anointed let me be with deadly venom 61
And die ere men can say, 'God save the queen !'

QUEEN ELIZABETH
Go, go, poor soul ! I envy not thy glory.
To feed my humor wish thyself no harm.

ANNE
No ? Why ! when he that is my husband now
Came to me as I followed Henry's corse,
When scarce the blood was well washed from his hands
Which issuèd from my other angel husband
And that dear saint which then I weeping followed –
O, when, I say, I looked on Richard's face,
This was my wish : 'Be thou,' quoth I, 'accursed
For making me, so young, so old a widow ! 72

---

48 *Take . . . hours* i.e. make full use of your head start 49 *You . . . me* i.e. I
will have letters written 50 *to . . . way* (supply 'telling him' before 'to') 51
ta'en taken, caught 52 *ill-dispersing* misfortune-scattering 54 *cockatrice*
basilisk (see I, ii, 150) 58 *inclusive verge* surrounding circle (i.e. the crown,
with reference to the band of red-hot steel sometimes placed as punishment
on the heads of traitors) 61 *Anointed* (anointing with holy oil was part of
the ceremony of coronation) 72 *so young . . . widow* (being so young she will
be a widow for a long time before she too dies)

And when thou wed'st, let sorrow haunt thy bed;
And be thy wife, if any be so mad,
More miserable by the life of thee
Than thou hast made me by my dear lord's death!'
Lo, ere I can repeat this curse again,
Within so small a time, my woman's heart
Grossly grew captive to his honey words
And proved the subject of mine own soul's curse,
Which hitherto hath held mine eyes from rest;
For never yet one hour in his bed
83   Did I enjoy the golden dew of sleep,
84   But with his timorous dreams was still awaked.
      Besides, he hates me for my father Warwick.
      And will (no doubt) shortly be rid of me.

QUEEN ELIZABETH
87   Poor heart, adieu! I pity thy complaining.

ANNE
      No more than with my soul I mourn for yours.

DORSET
      Farewell, thou woeful welcomer of glory.

ANNE
      Adieu, poor soul, that tak'st thy leave of it.

DUCHESS OF YORK [to Dorset]
      Go thou to Richmond, and good fortune guide thee!
         [To Anne]
      Go thou to Richard, and good angels tend thee!
         [To Queen Elizabeth]
      Go thou to sanctuary, and good thoughts possess thee!
      I to my grave, where peace and rest lie with me!
      Eighty odd years of sorrow have I seen,
96   And each hour's joy wracked with a week of teen.

QUEEN ELIZABETH
      Stay, yet look back with me unto the Tower.
      Pity, you ancient stones, those tender babes

---

83 *golden dew* i.e. precious refreshment   84 *timorous* full of fear; *still* continuously   87 *complaining* cause for complaint   96 *wracked* destroyed; *teen* grief

Whom envy hath immured within your walls –
Rough cradle for such little pretty ones !
Rude ragged nurse, old sullen playfellow
For tender princes – use my babies well !
So foolish sorrows bids your stones farewell.   *Exeunt.*

*

Sound a sennet. Enter Richard [as King], in pomp,   IV, ii
Buckingham, Catesby, Ratcliffe, Lovel [, a Page,
and others].

KING RICHARD
Stand all apart. Cousin of Buckingham –
BUCKINGHAM
My gracious sovereign ?
KING RICHARD
Give me thy hand.
          Sound. [Here he ascendeth the throne.]
                    Thus high, by thy advice
And thy assistance, is King Richard seated :
But shall we wear these glories for a day ?
Or shall they last, and we rejoice in them ?
BUCKINGHAM
Still live they, and for ever let them last !
KING RICHARD
Ah, Buckingham, now do I play the touch,   8
To try if thou be current gold indeed :
Young Edward lives. Think now what I would speak.
BUCKINGHAM
Say on, my loving lord.
KING RICHARD
Why, Buckingham, I say I would be king.
BUCKINGHAM
Why, so you are, my thrice-renownèd liege.

IV, ii The royal palace s.d. *sennet* a special set of notes on the trumpet
used for entrance and exit of processions 8 *touch* touchstone (a means of
testing gold)

KING RICHARD
Ha! Am I king? 'Tis so. But Edward lives.

BUCKINGHAM
True, noble prince.

15 **KING RICHARD**   O bitter consequence,
That Edward still should live true noble prince!
Cousin, thou wast not wont to be so dull.
Shall I be plain? I wish the bastards dead,
And I would have it suddenly performed.
What say'st thou now? Speak suddenly, be brief.

BUCKINGHAM
Your grace may do your pleasure.

KING RICHARD
Tut, tut, thou art all ice; thy kindness freezes.
Say, have I thy consent that they shall die?

BUCKINGHAM
Give me some little breath, some pause, dear lord,
Before I positively speak in this:
26 I will resolve you herein presently.   *Exit Buck[ingham].*

CATESBY *[aside to another]*
The king is angry. See, he gnaws his lip.

KING RICHARD
28 I will converse with iron-witted fools
And unrespective boys. None are for me
30 That look into me with considerate eyes.
High-reaching Buckingham grows circumspect.
Boy!

PAGE
My lord?

KING RICHARD
Know'st thou not any whom corrupting gold
Will tempt unto a close exploit of death?

PAGE
I know a discontented gentleman

15 *consequence* conclusion 26 *presently* at once 28–29 *iron-witted* . . .
unrespective unfeeling . . . thoughtless 30 *considerate* (eyes) which weigh
my motives, thoughtful

Whose humble means match not his haughty spirit :
Gold were as good as twenty orators,
And will, no doubt, tempt him to anything.

KING RICHARD
What is his name ?

PAGE   His name, my lord, is Tyrrel.

KING RICHARD
I partly know the man. Go call him hither, boy.
                                   Exit [Page].

The deep-revolving witty Buckingham   42
No more shall be the neighbor to my counsels.
Hath he so long held out with me, untired,   44
And stops he now for breath ? Well, be it so.
     Enter Stanley [Earl of Derby].
How now, Lord Stanley ? What's the news ?

DERBY   Know, my loving lord,
The Marquess Dorset, as I hear, is fled
To Richmond in the parts where he abides.
     [Stands aside.]

KING RICHARD
Come hither, Catesby. Rumor it abroad
That Anne my wife is very grievous sick :
I will take order for her keeping close.   51
Inquire me out some mean poor gentleman,
Whom I will marry straight to Clarence' daughter.
The boy is foolish, and I fear not him.   54
Look how thou dream'st ! I say again, give out
That Anne, my queen, is sick and like to die.
About it ! for it stands me much upon   57
To stop all hopes whose growth may damage me.
                                   [Exit Catesby.]

I must be married to my brother's daughter,
Or else my kingdom stands on brittle glass :
Murder her brothers, and then marry her –

42 *deep-revolving* profoundly politic   44 *held out* i.e. lasted the course   51
take . . . close make arrangements for her imprisonment   54 *foolish* i.e. an
idiot   57 *stands . . . upon* is of great importance to me

Uncertain way of gain ! But I am in
→ So far in blood that sin will pluck on sin.
64 Tear-falling pity dwells not in this eye.
Enter [Page, with] Tyrrel.
Is thy name Tyrrel ?

TYRREL
James Tyrrel, and your most obedient subject.

KING RICHARD
Art thou indeed ?

TYRREL   Prove me, my gracious lord.

KING RICHARD
Dar'st thou resolve to kill a friend of mine ?

TYRREL
69 Please you ;
But I had rather kill two enemies.

KING RICHARD
Why, there thou hast it ! Two deep enemies,
Foes to my rest and my sweet sleep's disturbers,
Are they that I would have thee deal upon :
Tyrrel, I mean those bastards in the Tower.

TYRREL
75 Let me have open means to come to them,
And soon I'll rid you from the fear of them.

KING RICHARD
Thou sing'st sweet music. Hark, come hither, Tyrrel.
Go, by this token. Rise, and lend thine ear.
Whispers.
There is no more but so : say it is done,
And I will love thee and prefer thee for it.

TYRREL
I will dispatch it straight.   *Exit.*
Enter Buckingham.

BUCKINGHAM
My lord, I have considered in my mind
The late request that you did sound me in.

---

64 *Tear-falling* i.e. weeping   69 *Please you* if it pleases you   75 *open* free

KING RICHARD
Well, let that rest. Dorset is fled to Richmond.

BUCKINGHAM
I hear the news, my lord.

KING RICHARD
Stanley, he is your wife's son. Well, look unto it.

BUCKINGHAM
My lord, I claim the gift, my due by promise,
For which your honor and your faith is pawned :
Th' earldom of Hereford and the moveables
Which you have promisèd I shall possess.   90

KING RICHARD
Stanley, look to your wife : if she convey
Letters to Richmond, you shall answer it.

BUCKINGHAM
What says your highness to my just request ?

KING RICHARD
I do remember me Henry the Sixth
Did prophesy that Richmond should be king
When Richmond was a little peevish boy.   96
A king ! – perhaps – [perhaps –

BUCKINGHAM
My lord –

KING RICHARD
How chance the prophet could not at that time
Have told me, I being by, that I should kill him ?

BUCKINGHAM
My lord, your promise for the earldom !

KING RICHARD
Richmond ! When last I was at Exeter,
The Mayor in courtesy showed me the castle,
And called it Rouge-mount ; at which name I started,   104
Because a bard of Ireland told me once   105
I should not live long after I saw Richmond.

96 *peevish* foolish   104 *Rouge-mount* i.e. Redhill (the incident is historical,
but the play on 'Richmond' is forced)   105 *bard* (the Celtic bards or poets
were also considered prophets)

BUCKINGHAM
My lord –
KING RICHARD
Ay, what's a clock?
BUCKINGHAM
I am thus bold to put your grace in mind
Of what you promised me.
KING RICHARD　　　　　　　Well, but what's a clock?
BUCKINGHAM
Upon the stroke of ten.
KING RICHARD　　　　　Well, let it strike.
BUCKINGHAM
Why let it strike?
KING RICHARD
113　Because that like a Jack thou keep'st the stroke
Betwixt thy begging and my meditation.
I am not in the giving vein to-day.]
BUCKINGHAM
116　May it please you to resolve me in my suit.
KING RICHARD
Thou troublest me; I am not in the vein.
　　　　　　　　　　　Exeunt [all but Buckingham].
BUCKINGHAM
And is it thus? Repays he my deep service
With such contempt? Made I him king for this?
O, let me think on Hastings, and be gone
121　To Brecknock while my fearful head is on!　　　Exit.

*

113 *Jack* a metal figure of a man which appeared to strike the hours in early
clocks (play on 'lowbred fellow'; cf. *begging*, l. 114)　113–14 *keep'st . . .
meditation* (like a Jack you) suspend the moment of striking (i.e. coming to
the point in your begging suit) and thus disturb my train of thought (so *let it
strike*, l. 111)　116 *resolve* i.e. give a final answer　121 *Brecknock* a manor
house in Wales; *fearful* full of fears

Enter Tyrrel.

TYRREL

The tyrannous and bloody act is done,
The most arch deed of piteous massacre 2
That ever yet this land was guilty of.
Dighton and Forrest, who I did suborn
To do this piece of ruthless butchery,
Albeit they were fleshed villains, bloody dogs,
Melted with tenderness and kind compassion, 7
Wept like to children in their death's sad story.
'O, thus,' quoth Dighton, 'lay the gentle babes.'
'Thus, thus,' quoth Forrest, 'girdling one another
Within their alablaster innocent arms. 11
Their lips were four red roses on a stalk,
Which in their summer beauty kissed each other.
A book of prayers on their pillow lay,
Which once,' quoth Forrest, 'almost changed my mind;
But O! the devil' – there the villain stopped;
When Dighton thus told on – 'We smotherèd
The most replenishèd sweet work of nature 18
That from the prime creation e'er she framèd.' 19
Hence both are gone with conscience and remorse:
They could not speak; and so I left them both,
To bear this tidings to the bloody king.
    Enter [King] Richard.
And here he comes. All health, my sovereign lord!

KING RICHARD

Kind Tyrrel, am I happy in thy news?

TYRREL

If to have done the thing you gave in charge 25
Beget your happiness, be happy then,
For it is done.

KING RICHARD But didst thou see them dead?

IV, iii The same 2 *most arch* chiefest 7 *kind* natural 11 *alablaster* white
(same as 'alabaster') 18 *replenishèd* complete (in the sense of being full of
virtues and beauty) 19 *prime* first 25 *done* i.e. had done

TYRREL
  I did, my lord.

KING RICHARD And buried, gentle Tyrrel?

TYRREL
  The chaplain of the Tower hath buried them;
  But where (to say the truth) I do not know.

KING RICHARD
  Come to me, Tyrrel, soon at after supper,
32 When thou shalt tell the process of their death.
  Meantime, but think how I may do thee good,
  And be inheritor of thy desire.
  Farewell till then.

TYRREL   I humbly take my leave.   *[Exit.]*

KING RICHARD
  The son of Clarence have I pent up close,
  His daughter meanly have I matched in marriage,
  The sons of Edward sleep in Abraham's bosom,
  And Anne my wife hath bid this world good night.
40 Now, for I know the Britain Richmond aims
  At young Elizabeth, my brother's daughter,
42 And by that knot looks proudly on the crown,
  To her go I, a jolly thriving wooer.
     Enter Ratcliffe.

RATCLIFFE
  My lord –

KING RICHARD
  Good or bad news, that thou com'st in so bluntly?

RATCLIFFE
  Bad news, my lord. Morton is fled to Richmond,
  And Buckingham, backed with the hardy Welshmen,
  Is in the field, and still his power increaseth.

KING RICHARD
  Ely with Richmond troubles me more near
  Than Buckingham and his rash-levied strength.

---

32 *process* story   40 *for* because; *Britain* Breton   42 *knot* i.e. marriage

Come! I have learned that fearful commenting   51
Is leaden servitor to dull delay;
Delay leads impotent and snail-paced beggary.   53
Then fiery expedition be my wing,   54
Jove's Mercury, and herald for a king!   55
Go, muster men. My counsel is my shield;
We must be brief when traitors brave the field.   *Exeunt.*

*

Enter old Queen Margaret.   IV, iv

QUEEN MARGARET
So now prosperity begins to mellow   1
And drop into the rotten mouth of death.
Here in these confines slily have I lurked
To watch the waning of mine enemies.
A dire induction am I witness to,   5
And will to France, hoping the consequence   6
Will prove as bitter, black, and tragical.
Withdraw thee, wretched Margaret! Who comes here?
                                            [Retires.]
        Enter Duchess [of York] and Queen [Elizabeth].

QUEEN ELIZABETH
Ah, my poor princes! ah, my tender babes!
My unblown flowers, new-appearing sweets!   10
If yet your gentle souls fly in the air
And be not fixed in doom perpetual,   12
Hover about me with your airy wings
And hear your mother's lamentation!

51–52 *fearful . . . servitor* timorous talk is the sluggish attendant   53 *beggary* ruin   54 *expedition* speed   55 *Mercury* messenger of the gods (note Richard's neat equation of himself with Jove, king of the gods)
IV, iv Before the royal palace   1–2 *So . . . death* (image taken from ripe fruit falling and rotting on the ground)   5 *induction* beginning (as of a play)   6 *consequence* conclusion (as the catastrophe of a play)   10 *sweets* fragrant flowers   12 *fixed . . . perpetual* i.e. assigned by God's judgment to their final place of punishment or reward

QUEEN MARGARET *[aside]*
   Hover about her. Say that right for right
   Hath dimmed your infant morn to agèd night.

DUCHESS OF YORK
17   So many miseries have crazed my voice
   That my woe-wearied tongue is still and mute.
   Edward Plantagenet, why art thou dead?

QUEEN MARGARET *[aside]*
20   Plantagenet doth quit Plantagenet;
21   Edward for Edward pays a dying debt.

QUEEN ELIZABETH
   Wilt thou, O God, fly from such gentle lambs
   And throw them in the entrails of the wolf?
24   When didst thou sleep when such a deed was done?

QUEEN MARGARET *[aside]*
   When holy Harry died, and my sweet son.

DUCHESS OF YORK
26   Dead life, blind sight, poor mortal-living ghost,
27   Woe's scene, world's shame, grave's due by life usurped,
28   Brief abstract and record of tedious days,
   Rest thy unrest on England's lawful earth,
      [Sits down.]
   Unlawfully made drunk with innocent blood!

QUEEN ELIZABETH
   Ah that thou wouldst as soon afford a grave
   As thou canst yield a melancholy seat!
   Then would I hide my bones, not rest them here.
   Ah, who hath any cause to mourn but we?
      [Sits down by her.]

QUEEN MARGARET *[comes forward]*
   If ancient sorrow be most reverent,
36   Give mine the benefit of seniory

---

17 *crazed* cracked   **20** *quit* make up for   **21** *dying debt* i.e. a debt for which
the payment is death   **24** *When* when ever (before this time)   **26** *mortal-
living* dead-alive   **27** *grave's . . . usurped* i.e. a dead body tyrannized over by
life   **28** *Brief abstract* epitome ('brief' may also be intended to limit
'record')   **36** *seniory* seniority

And let my griefs frown on the upper hand.   37
If sorrow can admit society,
      [Sits down with them.]
[Tell over your woes again by viewing mine].   39
I had an Edward, till a Richard killed him ;
I had a Harry, till a Richard killed him :
Thou hadst an Edward, till a Richard killed him ;
Thou hadst a Richard, till a Richard killed him.

DUCHESS OF YORK
I had a Richard too, and thou didst kill him ;
I had a Rutland too, thou holp'st to kill him.   45

QUEEN MARGARET
Thou hadst a Clarence too, and Richard killed him.
From forth the kennel of thy womb hath crept
A hellhound that doth hunt us all to death :
That dog, that had his teeth before his eyes,
To worry lambs and lap their gentle blood,
That foul defacer of God's handiwork,
That excellent grand tyrant of the earth   52
That reigns in gallèd eyes of weeping souls,   53
Thy womb let loose to chase us to our graves.
O upright, just, and true-disposing God,
How do I thank thee that this carnal cur   56
Preys on the issue of his mother's body
And makes her pew-fellow with others' moan !   58

DUCHESS OF YORK
O Harry's wife, triumph not in my woes !
God witness with me, I have wept for thine.

QUEEN MARGARET
Bear with me ! I am hungry for revenge,
And now I cloy me with beholding it.
Thy Edward he is dead, that killed my Edward ;

---

37 *frown . . . hand* i.e. have the mastery in looking grim or dismal   39 *Tell over* count   45 *holp'st* helpedest   52 *excellent* pre-eminently   53 *reigns . . . souls* i.e. flourishes (as a ruler) upon the tears wept from sore eyes of those individuals (whom he has injured)   56 *carnal* carnivorous   58 *pew-fellow* companion

64   Thy other Edward dead, to quit my Edward ;
65   Young York he is but boot, because both they
       Matched not the high perfection of my loss.
       Thy Clarence he is dead that stabbed my Edward,
       And the beholders of this frantic play,
69   Th' adulterate Hastings, Rivers, Vaughan, Grey,
       Untimely smoth'red in their dusky graves.
71   Richard yet lives, hell's black intelligencer ;
72   Only reserved their factor to buy souls
       And send them thither. But at hand, at hand,
       Ensues his piteous and unpitied end.
75   Earth gapes, hell burns, fiends roar, saints pray,
       To have him suddenly conveyed from hence.
       Cancel his bond of life, dear God, I pray,
       That I may live and say, 'The dog is dead.'

QUEEN ELIZABETH
       O, thou didst prophesy the time would come
       That I should wish for thee to help me curse
       That bottled spider, that foul bunch-backed toad !

QUEEN MARGARET
       I called thee then vain flourish of my fortune ;
       I called thee then poor shadow, painted queen,
       The presentation of but what I was,
85   The flattering index of a direful pageant,
       One heaved a-high to be hurled down below,
       A mother only mocked with two fair babes,
88   A dream of what thou wast, a garish flag,
       To be the aim of every dangerous shot ;
       A sign of dignity, a breath, a bubble,
91   A queen in jest, only to fill the scene.

---

64 *quit* redeem   65 *but boot* i.e. thrown in as an extra   69 *adulterate* guilty
of adultery   71 *intelligencer* secret agent   72 *Only . . . factor* above all others
chosen as their agent   75–77 *Earth . . . pray* (Shakespeare seems to be
thinking of the conclusion of Marlowe's *Doctor Faustus*)   85 *index* prologue ; *pageant* play or show   88–89 *garish . . . shot* brightly colored
standard-bearer (an appearance only, thus picking up *painted queen*, l. 83)
who draws the fire of all enemies   91 *queen . . . scene* i.e. a mute player-queen

Where is thy husband now? Where be thy brothers?
Where be thy two sons? Wherein dost thou joy?
Who sues and kneels and says, 'God save the queen'?
Where be the bending peers that flatterèd thee?
Where be the thronging troops that followèd thee?
Decline all this, and see what now thou art:　　　97
For happy wife, a most distressèd widow;
For joyful mother, one that wails the name;
For one being sued to, one that humbly sues;
For queen, a very caitiff crowned with care;　　　101
For she that scorned at me, now scorned of me;
For she being feared of all, now fearing one;
For she commanding all, obeyed of none.
Thus hath the course of justice whirled about
And left thee but a very prey to time,
Having no more but thought of what thou wast,
To torture thee the more, being what thou art.
Thou didst usurp my place, and dost thou not
Usurp the just proportion of my sorrow?
Now thy proud neck bears half my burdened yoke,　　　111
From which even here I slip my weary head
And leave the burden of it all on thee.
Farewell, York's wife, and queen of sad mischance!
These English woes shall make me smile in France.

QUEEN ELIZABETH
O thou well skilled in curses, stay awhile
And teach me how to curse mine enemies!

QUEEN MARGARET
Forbear to sleep the nights, and fast the days;
Compare dead happiness with living woe;
Think that thy babes were sweeter than they were
And he that slew them fouler than he is:
Bett'ring thy loss makes the bad causer worse;　　　122
Revolving this will teach thee how to curse.

97 *Decline* run through in order (as in a paradigm)　101 *caitiff* wretch　111
burdened burdensome　122 *Bett'ring . . . worse* i.e. magnifying thy loss
makes the perpetrator of the evil appear even worse than he is

QUEEN ELIZABETH

124 My words are dull. O, quicken them with thine!

QUEEN MARGARET

 Thy woes will make them sharp and pierce like mine.

       Exit [Queen] Margaret.

DUCHESS OF YORK

 Why should calamity be full of words?

QUEEN ELIZABETH

127 Windy attorneys to their client's woes,

128 Airy succeeders of intestate joys,

 Poor breathing orators of miseries,

 Let them have scope! Though what they will impart

 Help nothing else, yet do they ease the heart.

DUCHESS OF YORK

 If so, then be not tongue-tied: go with me,

 And in the breath of bitter words let's smother

 My damnèd son that thy two sweet sons smothered.

 The trumpet sounds. Be copious in exclaims.

  Enter King Richard and his Train [marching, with

  Drums and Trumpets].

KING RICHARD

136 Who intercepts me in my expedition?

DUCHESS OF YORK

 O, she that might have intercepted thee,

 By strangling thee in her accursèd womb,

 From all the slaughters (wretch!) that thou hast done!

QUEEN ELIZABETH

 Hid'st thou that forehead with a golden crown

 Where should be branded, if that right were right,

142 The slaughter of the prince that owed that crown

 And the dire death of my poor sons and brothers?

---

124 *quicken* put life into **127** *Windy . . . woes* (words are) airy pleaders for the
woes of their client (i.e. the one suffering) **128** *succeeders . . . joys* heirs of
joys which died without issue (folio reading 'intestine' [inward] may possibly be right; 'intestate' from quartos) **136** *expedition* (1) military under-
taking, (2) haste **142** *owed* possessed by right

Tell me, thou villain-slave, where are my children?   144
DUCHESS OF YORK
Thou toad, thou toad, where is thy brother Clarence?
And little Ned Plantagenet, his son?
QUEEN ELIZABETH
Where is the gentle Rivers, Vaughan, Grey?
DUCHESS OF YORK
Where is kind Hastings?
KING RICHARD
A flourish, trumpets! Strike alarum, drums!
Let not the heavens hear these telltale women
Rail on the Lord's anointed. Strike, I say!
  Flourish. Alarums.
Either be patient and entreat me fair,
Or with the clamorous report of war
Thus will I drown your exclamations.
DUCHESS OF YORK
Art thou my son?
KING RICHARD
Ay, I thank God, my father, and yourself.
DUCHESS OF YORK
Then patiently hear my impatience.
KING RICHARD
Madam, I have a touch of your condition   158
That cannot brook the accent of reproof.   159
DUCHESS OF YORK
O, let me speak!
KING RICHARD Do then, but I'll not hear. ←
DUCHESS OF YORK
I will be mild and gentle in my words.
KING RICHARD
And brief, good mother, for I am in haste.
DUCHESS OF YORK
Art thou so hasty? I have stayed for thee   163

---

144 *villain-slave* lowest criminal (with suggestions of 'lowbred' in 'villain'
[serf] and 'slave')   **158** *condition* temperament   **159** *accent* language   **163**
stayed waited

> (God knows) in torment and in agony.

KING RICHARD
> And came I not at last to comfort you?

DUCHESS OF YORK
166   No, by the Holy Rood, thou know'st it well,
  Thou cam'st on earth to make the earth my hell.
  A grievous burden was thy birth to me;
169   Tetchy and wayward was thy infancy;
170   Thy schooldays frightful, desp'rate, wild, and furious;
  Thy prime of manhood daring, bold, and venturous;
172   Thy age confirmed, proud, subtle, sly, and bloody,
  More mild, but yet more harmful – kind in hatred.
  What comfortable hour canst thou name
  That ever graced me with thy company?

KING RICHARD
176   Faith, none, but Humphrey Hour, that called your grace
  To breakfast once, forth of my company.
178   If I be so disgracious in your eye,
  Let me march on and not offend you, madam.
  Strike up the drum.

DUCHESS OF YORK   I prithee hear me speak.

KING RICHARD
> You speak too bitterly.

DUCHESS OF YORK   Hear me a word;
  For I shall never speak to thee again.

KING RICHARD
> So.

DUCHESS OF YORK
> Either thou wilt die by God's just ordinance
> Ere from this war thou turn a conqueror,
> Or I with grief and extreme age shall perish
> And never more behold thy face again.

---

166 *Holy Rood* Christ's cross   169 *Tetchy and wayward* fretful and willful
170 *frightful* full of fears   172 *age confirmed* i.e. having reached full maturity
176 *Humphrey Hour* (meaning uncertain; perhaps 'that hour when you
were paradoxically without food' [cf. 'dining with Duke Humphrey': going
hungry])   178 *disgracious* unpleasing

Therefore take with thee my most grievous curse,
Which in the day of battle tire thee more
Than all the complete armor that thou wear'st!   190
My prayers on the adverse party fight,
And there the little souls of Edward's children
Whisper the spirits of thine enemies
And promise them success and victory!
Bloody thou art, bloody will be thy end;
Shame serves thy life and doth thy death attend.   *Exit.*

QUEEN ELIZABETH
Though far more cause, yet much less spirit to curse
Abides in me. I say amen to her.

KING RICHARD
Stay, madam; I must talk a word with you.

QUEEN ELIZABETH
I have no moe sons of the royal blood   200
For thee to slaughter. For my daughters, Richard,
They shall be praying nuns, not weeping queens;
And therefore level not to hit their lives.   203

KING RICHARD
You have a daughter called Elizabeth,
Virtuous and fair, royal and gracious.

QUEEN ELIZABETH
And must she die for this? O, let her live,
And I'll corrupt her manners, stain her beauty,   207
Slander myself as false to Edward's bed,
Throw over her the veil of infamy:
So she may live unscarred of bleeding slaughter,
I will confess she was not Edward's daughter.

KING RICHARD
Wrong not her birth; she is a royal princess.

QUEEN ELIZABETH
To save her life, I'll say she is not so.

---

190 *complete armor* i.e. a full suit of armor, from head to foot   200 *moe* more
(in number)   203 *level . . . lives* i.e. do not take aim to kill them   207 *manners*
moral character

KING RICHARD

214　Her life is safest only in her birth.

QUEEN ELIZABETH

And only in that safety died her brothers.

KING RICHARD

Lo, at their birth good stars were opposite.

QUEEN ELIZABETH

217　No, to their lives ill friends were contrary.

KING RICHARD

218　All unavoided is the doom of destiny.

QUEEN ELIZABETH

219　True, when avoided grace makes destiny :

My babes were destined to a fairer death

If grace had blessed thee with a fairer life.

KING RICHARD

You speak as if that I had slain my cousins !

QUEEN ELIZABETH

223　Cousins indeed, and by their uncle cozened

Of comfort, kingdom, kindred, freedom, life :

225　Whose hand soever lanched their tender hearts,

226　Thy head (all indirectly) gave direction.

No doubt the murd'rous knife was dull and blunt

Till it was whetted on thy stone-hard heart

To revel in the entrails of my lambs.

230　But that still use of grief makes wild grief tame,

My tongue should to thy ears not name my boys

Till that my nails were anchored in thine eyes ;

233　And I, in such a desp'rate bay of death,

Like a poor bark of sails and tackling reft,

Rush all to pieces on thy rocky bosom.

KING RICHARD

Madam, so thrive I in my enterprise

214 *only* above all else　217 *contrary* opposed　218 *unavoided* unavoidable;
doom lot　219 *avoided grace* one who has rejected God's prevenient grace
(i.e. Richard)　223 *cozened* cheated or betrayed　225 *lanched* pierced　226
all indirectly i.e. even if not in express terms　230 *But that still* except that
continual　233 *bay* inlet (with play on the hunting term 'at bay' : driven to a
last stand)

And dangerous success of bloody wars
As I intend more good to you and yours
Than ever you or yours by me were harmed!

QUEEN ELIZABETH
What good is covered with the face of heaven,   240
To be discovered, that can do me good?

KING RICHARD
Th' advancement of your children, gentle lady.

QUEEN ELIZABETH
Up to some scaffold, there to lose their heads!

KING RICHARD
Unto the dignity and height of fortune,
The high imperial type of this earth's glory.   245

QUEEN ELIZABETH
Flatter my sorrow with report of it:
Tell me, what state, what dignity, what honor
Canst thou demise to any child of mine?   248

KING RICHARD
Even all I have – ay, and myself and all –
Will I withal endow a child of thine,   250
So in the Lethe of thy angry soul   251
Thou drown the sad remembrance of those wrongs
Which thou supposest I have done to thee.

QUEEN ELIZABETH
Be brief, lest that the process of thy kindness
Last longer telling than thy kindness' date.

KING RICHARD
Then know that from my soul I love thy daughter.   256

QUEEN ELIZABETH
My daughter's mother thinks it with her soul.

KING RICHARD
What do you think?

240 *What . . . heaven* i.e. what good is yet to be found in this world (not already discovered)   245 *imperial type* symbol of rule   248 *demise* transmit   250 *withal* with   251 *Lethe* a river in Hell (to drink of which induced forgetfulness)   256 *from my soul* with my very soul (but Queen Elizabeth takes Richard to mean that his love is 'from' [i.e. separated from] his inmost feelings)

QUEEN ELIZABETH
> That thou dost love my daughter from thy soul.
> So from thy soul's love didst thou love her brothers,
> And from my heart's love I do thank thee for it.

KING RICHARD
> Be not so hasty to confound my meaning:
> I mean that with my soul I love thy daughter
> And do intend to make her Queen of England.

QUEEN ELIZABETH
> Well then, who dost thou mean shall be her king?

KING RICHARD
> Even he that makes her queen. Who should be else?

QUEEN ELIZABETH
> What, thou?

KING RICHARD Even so. How think you of it?

QUEEN ELIZABETH
> How canst thou woo her?

KING RICHARD   That would I learn of you,
269 As one being best acquainted with her humor.

QUEEN ELIZABETH
> And wilt thou learn of me?

KING RICHARD   Madam, with all my heart.

QUEEN ELIZABETH
> Send to her by the man that slew her brothers
> A pair of bleeding hearts; thereon engrave
> 'Edward' and 'York'; then haply will she weep:
> Therefore present to her – as sometimes Margaret
> Did to thy father, steeped in Rutland's blood –
> A handkercher, which say to her did drain
> The purple sap from her sweet brother's body,
278 And bid her wipe her weeping eyes withal.
> If this inducement move her not to love,
> Send her a letter of thy noble deeds:
> Tell her thou mad'st away her uncle Clarence,
> Her uncle Rivers; ay (and for her sake!),

269 *humor* temperament   278 *withal* with (it)

Mad'st quick conveyance with her good aunt Anne.   283

KING RICHARD
  You mock me, madam ; this is not the way
  To win your daughter.

QUEEN ELIZABETH   There is no other way,
  Unless thou couldst put on some other shape,
  And not be Richard that hath done all this.

KING RICHARD
  Say that I did all this for love of her.

QUEEN ELIZABETH
  Nay, then indeed she cannot choose but hate thee,
  Having bought love with such a bloody spoil.   290

KING RICHARD
  Look what is done cannot be now amended :   291
  Men shall deal unadvisedly sometimes,
  Which after-hours gives leisure to repent.
  If I did take the kingdom from your sons,
  To make amends I'll give it to your daughter ;
  If I have killed the issue of your womb,
  To quicken your increase I will beget   297
  Mine issue of your blood upon your daughter.
  A grandam's name is little less in love
  Than is the doting title of a mother ;
  They are as children but one step below,
  Even of your metal, of your very blood,   302
  Of all one pain, save for a night of groans
  Endured of her for whom you bid like sorrow :   304
  Your children were vexation to your youth,
  But mine shall be a comfort to your age.
  The loss you have is but a son being king,
  And by that loss your daughter is made queen.
  I cannot make you what amends I would ;

283 *quick conveyance with* speedy removal of   290 *spoil* slaughter (hunting
term : the breaking up of the quarry after the kill)   291 *Look what* whatever
297 *quicken your increase* i.e. give new life to your (dead) offspring   302
metal substance   304 *of* by ; *bid* underwent, suffered

310   Therefore accept such kindness as I can.
311   Dorset your son, that with a fearful soul
      Leads discontented steps in foreign soil,
      This fair alliance quickly shall call home
      To high promotions and great dignity.
      The king, that calls your beauteous daughter wife,
      Familiarly shall call thy Dorset brother :
      Again shall you be mother to a king,
      And all the ruins of distressful times
      Repaired with double riches of content.
      What ! we have many goodly days to see :
      The liquid drops of tears that you have shed
322   Shall come again, transformed to orient pearl,
323   Advantaging their love with interest
      Of ten times double gain of happiness.
      Go then, my mother ; to thy daughter go ;
      Make bold her bashful years with your experience ;
      Prepare her ears to hear a wooer's tale ;
      Put in her tender heart th' aspiring flame
      Of golden sovereignty ; acquaint the princess
      With the sweet silent hours of marriage joys ;
      And when this arm of mine hath chastisèd
      The petty rebel, dull-brained Buckingham,
333   Bound with triumphant garlands will I come
      And lead thy daughter to a conqueror's bed ;
335   To whom I will retail my conquest won,
      And she shall be sole victoress, Caesar's Caesar.

QUEEN ELIZABETH
      What were I best to say ? Her father's brother
      Would be her lord ? Or shall I say her uncle ?
      Or he that slew her brothers and her uncles ?
      Under what title shall I woo for thee

---

310 *can* i.e. am able to give   311 *fearful* full of fears   322 *orient* shining
323 *love* i.e. the love which gave rise to the tears   333 *triumphant garlands*
i.e. garlands befitting a military triumph (in the Roman sense)   335 *retail*
recount (though Shakespeare would seem to mean 'transmit')

That God, the law, my honor, and her love
Can make seem pleasing to her tender years?

KING RICHARD
Infer fair England's peace by this alliance.   343

QUEEN ELIZABETH
Which she shall purchase with still-lasting war.

KING RICHARD
Tell her the king, that may command, entreats.

QUEEN ELIZABETH
That at her hands which the king's King forbids.

KING RICHARD
Say she shall be a high and mighty queen.

QUEEN ELIZABETH
To vail the title, as her mother doth.   348

KING RICHARD
Say I will love her everlastingly.

QUEEN ELIZABETH
But how long shall that title 'ever' last?

KING RICHARD
Sweetly in force unto her fair life's end.

QUEEN ELIZABETH
But how long fairly shall her sweet life last?

KING RICHARD
As long as heaven and nature lengthens it.

QUEEN ELIZABETH
As long as hell and Richard likes of it.

KING RICHARD
Say I, her sovereign, am her subject low.

QUEEN ELIZABETH
But she, your subject, loathes such sovereignty.   356

KING RICHARD
Be eloquent in my behalf to her.

QUEEN ELIZABETH
An honest tale speeds best being plainly told.

---

343 *Infer* imply   348 *vail* abase, lower (quarto reading 'wail' is perhaps
preferable)   356 *sovereignty* (1) rule, (2) ruler (i.e. Richard)

KING RICHARD
Then plainly to her tell my loving tale.
QUEEN ELIZABETH
360 Plain and not honest is too harsh a style.
KING RICHARD
Your reasons are too shallow and too quick.
QUEEN ELIZABETH
O no, my reasons are too deep and dead –
Too deep and dead (poor infants) in their graves.
KING RICHARD
Harp not on that string, madam ; that is past.
QUEEN ELIZABETH
Harp on it still shall I till heartstrings break.
KING RICHARD
366 Now, by my George, my garter, and my crown –
QUEEN ELIZABETH
Profaned, dishonored, and the third usurped.
KING RICHARD
I swear –
QUEEN ELIZABETH By nothing, for this is no oath :
Thy George, profaned, hath lost his lordly honor ;
Thy garter, blemished, pawned his knightly virtue ;
Thy crown, usurped, disgraced his kingly glory.
If something thou wouldst swear to be believed,
Swear then by something that thou hast not wronged.
KING RICHARD
Then by myself –
QUEEN ELIZABETH Thyself is self-misused.
KING RICHARD
Now by the world –
QUEEN ELIZABETH 'Tis full of thy foul wrongs.

360 *Plain . . . style* i.e. plain style (cf. the proverb 'Truth is plain') unless it is sincere will be too harsh; lies (i.e. things not honest) need the decorated style   366 *George . . . garter* (a jewelled pendant with the figure of St George and the gold collar from which it hung were parts of the insignia of the Order of the Garter)

KING RICHARD
My father's death –
QUEEN ELIZABETH Thy life hath it dishonored.
KING RICHARD
Why then, by God –
QUEEN ELIZABETH   God's wrong is most of all :
If thou didst fear to break an oath with him,
The unity the king my husband made   379
Thou hadst not broken, nor my brothers died.
If thou hadst feared to break an oath by him,
Th' imperial metal, circling now thy head,   382
Had graced the tender temples of my child,
And both the princes had been breathing here,
Which now, two tender bedfellows for dust,
Thy broken faith hath made the prey for worms.
What canst thou swear by now ?
KING RICHARD   The time to come.
QUEEN ELIZABETH
That thou hast wrongèd in the time o'erpast ;
For I myself have many tears to wash
Hereafter time, for time past wronged by thee.   390
The children live whose fathers thou hast slaughtered,
Ungoverned youth, to wail it in their age ;   392
The parents live whose children thou hast butchered,
Old barren plants, to wail it with their age.
Swear not by time to come, for that thou hast
Misused ere used, by times ill-used o'erpast.
KING RICHARD
As I intend to prosper and repent,   397
So thrive I in my dangerous affairs
Of hostile arms ! Myself myself confound !
Heaven and fortune bar me happy hours !

379 *unity* (the 'reconciliation' in II, i)   382 *imperial metal* i.e. royal crown
390 *Hereafter* future   392 *Ungoverned* i.e. without parents   397–98 *As . . .
So* to the degree I mean to do well and repent, to such a degree   397–405 *As
. . . daughter* (note that Richard here in effect curses himself, bringing the
curses in this scene to a final focus)

Day, yield me not thy light, nor, night, thy rest!
Be opposite all planets of good luck
To my proceeding if, with dear heart's love,
Immaculate devotion, holy thoughts,
I tender not thy beauteous princely daughter!
In her consists my happiness and thine;
Without her, follows to myself and thee,
Herself, the land, and many a Christian soul,
Death, desolation, ruin, and decay.
410 It cannot be avoided but by this;
It will not be avoided but by this.
Therefore, dear mother (I must call you so),
Be the attorney of my love to her:
Plead what I will be, not what I have been –
Not my deserts, but what I will deserve;
Urge the necessity and state of times,
417 And be not peevish-fond in great designs.

QUEEN ELIZABETH
Shall I be tempted of the devil thus?

KING RICHARD
Ay, if the devil tempt you to do good.

QUEEN ELIZABETH
420 Shall I forget myself to be myself?

KING RICHARD
Ay, if yourself's remembrance wrong yourself.

QUEEN ELIZABETH
Yet thou didst kill my children.

KING RICHARD
But in your daughter's womb I bury them,
Where, in that nest of spicery, they will breed
425 Selves of themselves, to your recomforture.

QUEEN ELIZABETH
Shall I go win my daughter to thy will?

417 *peevish-fond* foolishly self-willed (folio reading 'peevish found' may possibly be correct; Q1 reads 'peevish, fond') 420 *Shall . . . be myself* i.e. shall I forget who I am 425 *recomforture* consolation

KING RICHARD
　And be a happy mother by the deed.

QUEEN ELIZABETH
　I go. Write to me very shortly,
　And you shall understand from me her mind.

KING RICHARD
　Bear her my true love's kiss ; and so farewell –
　　　　　　　　　　　Exit Q[ueen Elizabeth].
→ Relenting fool, and shallow, changing woman !   431
　　　Enter Ratcliffe [, Catesby following].
　How now ? What news ?

RATCLIFFE
　Most mighty sovereign, on the western coast
　Rideth a puissant navy ; to our shores
　Throng many doubtful hollow-hearted friends,
　Unarmed, and unresolved to beat them back.   436
　'Tis thought that Richmond is their admiral ;   437
→And there they hull, expecting but the aid   438
　Of Buckingham to welcome them ashore.

KING RICHARD
　Some light-foot friend post to the Duke of Norfolk :
　Ratcliffe, thyself – or Catesby – where is he ?

CATESBY
　Here, my good lord.

KING RICHARD   Catesby, fly to the duke.

CATESBY
　I will, my lord, with all convenient haste.

KING RICHARD
　Ratcliffe, come hither. Post to Salisbury.
　When thou com'st thither –
　　　[To Catesby]   Dull unmindful villain,
　Why stay'st thou here and go'st not to the duke ?

CATESBY
　First, mighty liege, tell me your highness' pleasure,
　What from your grace I shall deliver to him.

431 *shallow* superficial　436 *unresolved* undetermined how to act　437 *their admiral* i.e. of the *navy* of l. 434　438 *hull* drift with the winds

KING RICHARD

O, true, good Catesby : bid him levy straight
The greatest strength and power that he can make
And meet me suddenly at Salisbury.

CATESBY

I go.   *Exit.*

RATCLIFFE

What, may it please you, shall I do at Salisbury ?

KING RICHARD

Why, what wouldst thou do there before I go ?

RATCLIFFE

455   Your highness told me I should post before.

KING RICHARD

My mind is changed.
    Enter Lord Stanley [Earl of Derby].
                        Stanley, what news with you ?

DERBY

None good, my liege, to please you with the hearing,
Nor none so bad but well may be reported.

KING RICHARD

Hoyday, a riddle ! Neither good nor bad !
What need'st thou run so many miles about,
When thou mayest tell thy tale the nearest way ?
Once more, what news ?

DERBY   Richmond is on the seas.

KING RICHARD

There let him sink, and be the seas on him !
464   White-livered runagate, what doth he there ?

DERBY

I know not, mighty sovereign, but by guess.

KING RICHARD

Well, as you guess ?

DERBY

Stirred up by Dorset, Buckingham, and Morton,
He makes for England, here to claim the crown.

---

455 *post* hasten   464 *runagate* vagabond or, perhaps, deserter (cf. V, iii, 317)

KING RICHARD

Is the chair empty? is the sword unswayed?   469
Is the king dead? the empire unpossessed?   470
What heir of York is there alive but we?
And who is England's king but great York's heir?
Then tell me, what makes he upon the seas?   473

DERBY

Unless for that, my liege, I cannot guess.

KING RICHARD

Unless for that he comes to be your liege,
You cannot guess wherefore the Welshman comes.
Thou wilt revolt and fly to him, I fear.

DERBY

No, my good lord; therefore mistrust me not.

KING RICHARD

Where is thy power then to beat him back?
Where be thy tenants and thy followers?
Are they not now upon the western shore,
Safe-conducting the rebels from their ships?

DERBY

No, my good lord, my friends are in the North.

KING RICHARD

Cold friends to me! What do they in the North   484
When they should serve their sovereign in the West?

DERBY

They have not been commanded, mighty king:
Pleaseth your majesty to give me leave,
I'll muster up my friends and meet your grace
Where and what time your majesty shall please.

KING RICHARD

Ay, thou wouldst be gone to join with Richmond:
But I'll not trust thee.

DERBY   Most mighty sovereign,
You have no cause to hold my friendship doubtful.

469 *sword* i.e. the sword of state, part of the king's regalia symbolic of power
470 *empire* kingdom (i.e. the thing requiring rule)   473 *makes he* is he doing
484 *Cold* chilling (with play on Derby's friends being in the North)

Buck true traitor

          I never was nor never will be false.

KING RICHARD
          Go then and muster men. But leave behind
          Your son, George Stanley. Look your heart be firm,
496   Or else his head's assurance is but frail.

DERBY
          So deal with him as I prove true to you.   *Exit.*
              Enter a Messenger.

1. MESSENGER
          My gracious sovereign, now in Devonshire,
499   As I by friends am well advertisèd,
500   Sir Edward Courtney and the haughty prelate,
          Bishop of Exeter, his elder brother,
502   With many moe confederates, are in arms.
              Enter another Messenger.

2. MESSENGER
503   In Kent, my liege, the Guildfords are in arms,
          And every hour more competitors
          Flock to the rebels, and their power grows strong.
              Enter another Messenger.

3. MESSENGER
          My lord, the army of great Buckingham –

KING RICHARD
507   Out on you, owls! Nothing but songs of death?
              He striketh him.
          There, take thou that, till thou bring better news.

3. MESSENGER
          The news I have to tell your majesty
          Is that by sudden floods and fall of waters
          Buckingham's army is dispersed and scattered,
          And he himself wand'red away alone,
          No man knows whither.
513 KING RICHARD   I cry thee mercy:

---

496 *head's assurance* i.e. that his head will not be cut off   499 *advertisèd*
informed   500, 503 *Courtney, Guildfords* (supporters of Buckingham)   502
moe more (in number)   507 *owls* (the hoot or song of the owl was frequently
believed to portend evil)   513 *cry thee mercy* beg your pardon

There is my purse to cure that blow of thine.
Hath any well-advisèd friend proclaimed   515
Reward to him that brings the traitor in?

3. MESSENGER
Such proclamation hath been made, my lord.
Enter another Messenger.

4. MESSENGER
Sir Thomas Lovel and Lord Marquess Dorset,   518
'Tis said, my liege, in Yorkshire are in arms.
But this good comfort bring I to your highness:
The Britain navy is dispersed by tempest;   521
Richmond in Dorsetshire sent out a boat
Unto the shore to ask those on the banks
If they were his assistants, yea or no;
Who answered him they came from Buckingham
Upon his party. He, mistrusting them,
Hoised sail, and made his course again for Britain.   527

KING RICHARD
March on, march on, since we are up in arms;
If not to fight with foreign enemies,
Yet to beat down these rebels here at home.
Enter Catesby.

CATESBY
My liege, the Duke of Buckingham is taken.
That is the best news. That the Earl of Richmond
Is with a mighty power landed at Milford
Is colder tidings, but yet they must be told.

KING RICHARD
Away towards Salisbury! While we reason here,
A royal battle might be won and lost.
Some one take order Buckingham be brought
To Salisbury; the rest march on with me.
                    Flourish. Exeunt.

*

515 *well-advisèd* foresighted   518 *Lovel* (supporter of Buckingham)   521
Britain Breton   527 *Hoised* hoisted; *Britain* Brittany

IV, v   *Enter [Lord Stanley Earl of] Derby, and*
        Sir Christopher [Urswick, a priest].

DERBY

    Sir Christopher, tell Richmond this from me:
    That in the sty of the most deadly boar
3   My son George Stanley is franked up in hold;
    If I revolt, off goes young George's head;
    The fear of that holds off my present aid.
    So get thee gone; commend me to thy lord.
    Withal say that the queen hath heartily consented
8   He should espouse Elizabeth her daughter.
    But tell me, where is princely Richmond now?

CHRISTOPHER

10   At Pembroke, or at Ha'rford-West in Wales.

DERBY

    What men of name resort to him?

CHRISTOPHER

    Sir Walter Herbert, a renownèd soldier,
    Sir Gilbert Talbot, Sir William Stanley,
14   Oxford, redoubted Pembroke, Sir James Blunt,
    And Rice ap Thomas, with a valiant crew,
    And many other of great name and worth;
    And towards London do they bend their power,
    If by the way they be not fought withal.

DERBY

    Well, hie thee to thy lord. I kiss his hand:
    My letter will resolve him of my mind.
        [Gives letter.]
    Farewell.   *Exeunt.*

*

IV, v Lord Stanley's house **s.d.** *Sir* (see III, ii, 109) **3** *franked up in hold*
shut up (as in a *sty*, l. 2) in custody (the *boar* in l. 2 being, of course, Richard)
8 *He . . . daughter* (Shakespeare's reference here to Richmond's projected
marriage with Princess Elizabeth makes it fairly certain that we should
interpret Queen Elizabeth's apparent capitulation to Richard in IV, iv, 426–
29 as a ruse to trick him) **10** *Pembroke* county in southwestern Wales (see
reference to the Pembroke family, l. 14); *Ha'rford-West* town in Pembroke
14 *redoubted* dreaded; *Pembroke* i.e. Jasper Tudor, Richmond's uncle

Enter Buckingham with Halberds [and the Sheriff],   V, i
led to execution.

BUCKINGHAM

Will not King Richard let me speak with him?

SHERIFF

No, my good lord; therefore be patient.

BUCKINGHAM

Hastings, and Edward's children, Grey and Rivers,
Holy King Henry and thy fair son Edward,
Vaughan and all that have miscarrièd
By underhand corrupted foul injustice,
If that your moody discontented souls   7
Do through the clouds behold this present hour,
Even for revenge mock my destruction!   9
This is All Souls' day, fellow, is it not?   10

SHERIFF

It is, my lord.

BUCKINGHAM

Why, then All Souls' day is my body's doomsday.   12
This is the day which in King Edward's time
I wished might fall on me when I was found
False to his children and his wife's allies;
This is the day wherein I wished to fall
By the false faith of him whom most I trusted;
This, this All Souls' day to my fearful soul   18
Is the determined respite of my wrongs: 19
That high All-seer which I dallied with
Hath turned my feignèd prayer on my head
And given in earnest what I begged in jest.
Thus doth He force the swords of wicked men

V, i An open place in Salisbury   7 *discontented souls* i.e. souls which could
not rest in peace until their violent deaths had been revenged   9 *Even for* i.e.
impelled by   10 *All Souls' day* November 2, the day on which the Roman
Catholic Church intercedes for all Christian souls   12 *doomsday* day of
final judgment (death being the sentence)   18 *fearful* terrified   19 *determined . . . wrongs* i.e. the foreordained moment past which no cessation (of
punishment) will be granted for all the wrongs I have committed

To turn their own points in their masters' bosoms;
Thus Margaret's curse falls heavy on my neck:
'When he,' quoth she, 'shall split thy heart with sorrow,
Remember Margaret was a prophetess.' –
Come lead me, officers, to the block of shame.
Wrong hath but wrong, and blame the due of blame.
Exeunt Buckingham with Officers.

*

V, ii   *Enter Richmond, Oxford, [Sir James] Blunt, [Sir*
            Walter] Herbert, and others, with Drum and Colors.

RICHMOND

Fellows in arms, and my most loving friends,
Bruised underneath the yoke of tyranny,
3   Thus far into the bowels of the land
Have we marched on without impediment;
5   And here receive we from our father Stanley
Lines of fair comfort and encouragement.
The wretched, bloody, and usurping boar,
That spoiled your summer fields and fruitful vines,
Swills your warm blood like wash, and makes his trough
10   In your embowelled bosoms – this foul swine
11   Is now even in the centry of this isle,
Near to the town of Leicester, as we learn:
From Tamworth thither is but one day's march.
In God's name cheerly on, courageous friends,
To reap the harvest of perpetual peace
By this one bloody trial of sharp war.

OXFORD

17   Every man's conscience is a thousand men,

V, ii A camp near Tamworth 3 *bowels* heart or center (Richmond's army
is at Tamworth, Staffordshire, on its way to the scene of the final battle
with Richard at Bosworth Field, Leicestershire; cf. ll. 12–13) 5 *our*
(royal plural); *father Stanley* (Richmond was the son of Edmund Tudor
and Margaret Beaufort; Lord Stanley, Earl of Derby, was his mother's
third husband) 10 *embowelled* disembowelled 11 *centry* center 17 *con-*
science i.e. his conscience tells him that he is on the 'right' side

To fight against this guilty homicide.

HERBERT
I doubt not but his friends will turn to us.

BLUNT
He hath no friends but what are friends for fear,
Which in his dearest need will fly from him.

RICHMOND
All for our vantage. Then in God's name march!
True hope is swift and flies with swallow's wings;
Kings it makes gods, and meaner creatures kings.

Exeunt omnes.

*

Enter King Richard in arms, with Norfolk, Ratcliffe,   V, iii
and the Earl of Surrey [, and Soldiers].

KING RICHARD
Here pitch our tent, even here in Bosworth field.
My Lord of Surrey, why look you so sad?   2

SURREY
My heart is ten times lighter than my looks.

KING RICHARD
My Lord of Norfolk –

NORFOLK   Here, most gracious liege.

KING RICHARD
Norfolk, we must have knocks. Ha! must we not?

NORFOLK
We must both give and take, my loving lord.

KING RICHARD
Up with my tent! Here will I lie to-night;
  [Soldiers begin to set up the King's tent.]
But where to-morrow? Well, all's one for that.   8
Who hath descried the number of the traitors?

NORFOLK
Six or seven thousand is their utmost power.

V, iii Bosworth Field   2 *sad* heavy-spirited   8 *all's . . . that* i.e. it makes
no difference

KING RICHARD

11 Why, our battalia trebles that account :
Besides, the king's name is a tower of strength,
13 Which they upon the adverse faction want.
Up with the tent ! Come, noble gentlemen,
15 Let us survey the vantage of the ground.
16 Call for some men of sound direction :
Let's lack no discipline, make no delay,
For, lords, to-morrow is a busy day.   *Exeunt.*
*Enter Richmond, Sir William Brandon, Oxford, and
Dorset [, Herbert, and Blunt. Some of the Soldiers
pitch Richmond's tent].*

RICHMOND

The weary sun hath made a golden set
20 And by the bright tract of his fiery car
Gives token of a goodly day to-morrow.
Sir William Brandon, you shall bear my standard.
Give me some ink and paper in my tent :
I'll draw the form and model of our battle,
Limit each leader to his several charge,
And part in just proportion our small power.
My Lord of Oxford, – you, Sir William Brandon, –
And you, Sir Walter Herbert – stay with me.
The Earl of Pembroke keeps his regiment ;
30 Good Captain Blunt, bear my good-night to him,
And by the second hour in the morning
Desire the earl to see me in my tent :
Yet one thing more, good captain, do for me –
Where is Lord Stanley quartered, do you know ?

BLUNT

Unless I have mista'en his colors much
(Which well I am assured I have not done),

---

11 *battalia* armed forces   13 *want* lack   15 *the vantage . . . ground* i.e. the
military advantages offered by the spot chosen for the battle   16 *of sound
direction* capable of giving sound orders   20 *tract* track ; *car* chariot (with
reference to the chariot of Phoebus, god of the sun)

His regiment lies half a mile at least
South from the mighty power of the king.

RICHMOND

If without peril it be possible,
Sweet Blunt, make some good means to speak with him   *40*
And give him from me this most needful note.

BLUNT

Upon my life, my lord, I'll undertake it ;
And so God give you quiet rest to-night !

RICHMOND

Good night, good Captain Blunt.   *[Exit Blunt.]*
                              Come, gentlemen,
Let us consult upon to-morrow's business.
In to my tent ; the dew is raw and cold.
                              They withdraw into the tent.
          Enter [, to his tent, King] Richard, Ratcliffe,
          Norfolk, and Catesby.

KING RICHARD

What is't a clock ?

CATESBY   It's supper time, my lord ;
It's nine a clock.   *48*

KING RICHARD   I will not sup to-night.
Give me some ink and paper.
What ? is my beaver easier than it was ?   *50*
And all my armor laid into my tent ?

CATESBY

It is, my liege ; and all things are in readiness.

KING RICHARD

Good Norfolk, hie thee to thy charge ;
Use careful watch, choose trusty sentinels.   *54*

NORFOLK

I go, my lord.

---

48 nine a clock (too late for an Elizabethan supper ; the 'six of clocke' of
Quarto 1 fits this context better, but is obviously too early for the time
indications in scene ii and later)   *50 beaver* face-guard of a helmet   *54*
Use careful watch i.e. see that a thorough alert is observed

KING RICHARD
Stir with the lark to-morrow, gentle Norfolk.

NORFOLK
I warrant you, my lord.   *Exit.*

KING RICHARD
Catesby!

CATESBY
My lord?

59 KING RICHARD Send out a pursuivant-at-arms
To Stanley's regiment; bid him bring his power
Before sunrising, lest his son George fall
Into the blind cave of eternal night.   *[Exit Catesby.]*

63 Fill me a bowl of wine. Give me a watch.
64 Saddle white Surrey for the field to-morrow.
65 Look that my staves be sound and not too heavy.
Ratcliffe!

RATCLIFFE
My lord?

KING RICHARD
Saw'st thou the melancholy Lord Northumberland?

RATCLIFFE
Thomas the Earl of Surrey and himself,
70 Much about cockshut time, from troop to troop
Went through the army, cheering up the soldiers.

KING RICHARD
So, I am satisfied. Give me a bowl of wine.
I have not that alacrity of spirit
Nor cheer of mind that I was wont to have.
      [Wine brought.]
Set it down. Is ink and paper ready?

RATCLIFFE
It is, my lord.

59 *pursuivant-at-arms* junior officer, attending on a herald   63 *a watch* a
special guard (cf. l. 77) or a timepiece   64 *white Surrey* (Richard entered
Leicester on a 'great white courser' [Holinshed], but the name is Shakespeare's and must not be confused with Surrey in l. 69)   65 *staves* lance
shafts   70 *cockshut time* evening twilight

KING RICHARD

    Bid my guard watch. Leave me. Ratcliffe,
    About the mid of night come to my tent
    And help to arm me. Leave me, I say.   *Exit Ratcliffe.*
                    [King Richard withdraws
                        into his tent, and sleeps.]
      Enter [Lord Stanley Earl of] Derby, to Richmond
      in his tent [, Lords and others attending].

DERBY

    Fortune and victory sit on thy helm!

RICHMOND

    All comfort that the dark night can afford
    Be to thy person, noble father-in-law!
    Tell me, how fares our loving mother?

DERBY

    I, by attorney, bless thee from thy mother,   84
    Who prays continually for Richmond's good:
    So much for that. The silent hours steal on
    And flaky darkness breaks within the east.   87
    In brief, for so the season bids us be,
    Prepare thy battle early in the morning   89
    And put thy fortune to the arbitrement
    Of bloody strokes and mortal-staring war.   91
    I, as I may – that which I would I cannot –
    With best advantage will deceive the time   93
    And aid thee in this doubtful shock of arms.
    But on thy side I may not be too forward,
    Lest, being seen, thy brother, tender George,
    Be executed in his father's sight.
    Farewell. The leisure and the fearful time   98
    Cuts off the ceremonious vows of love
    And ample interchange of sweet discourse

---

84 *attorney* proxy   87 *flaky darkness* i.e. darkness still flaked with light   89 *battle* armed forces (see *battalia*, l. 11 above)   91 *mortal-staring* killing (like the basilisk) with a glance of the eye   93 *With . . . time* i.e. will make the greatest profit of the moment without giving the appearance of doing so   98 *leisure . . . time* (lack of) time and the threat of the moment

Which so long sund'red friends should dwell upon.
God give us leisure for these rites of love!
Once more adieu : be valiant, and speed well!

RICHMOND

Good lords, conduct him to his regiment.
105 I'll strive with troublèd thoughts, to take a nap,
106 Lest leaden slumber peise me down to-morrow,
When I should mount with wings of victory :
Once more, good night, kind lords and gentlemen.

Exeunt. Manet Richmond.

O Thou, whose captain I account myself,
Look on my forces with a gracious eye ;
111 Put in their hands thy bruising irons of wrath,
That they may crush down with a heavy·fall
The usurping helmets of our adversaries ;
Make us thy ministers of chastisement,
That we may praise thee in the victory.
To thee I do commend my watchful soul
117 Ere I let fall the windows of mine eyes :
Sleeping and waking. O, defend me still!

Sleeps.
Enter the Ghost of Prince Edward, son to Henry the Sixth.

GHOST *(to Richard)*

Let me sit heavy on thy soul to-morrow!
Think how thou stab'st me in my prime of youth
At Tewkesbury : despair therefore, and die!
(To Richmond)
122 Be cheerful, Richmond ; for the wrongèd souls
Of butcherèd princes fight in thy behalf.
King Henry's issue, Richmond, comforts thee.
Enter the Ghost of Henry the Sixth.

GHOST *(to Richard)*
125 When I was mortal, my anointed body

---

105 *with troublèd thoughts* i.e. in spite of my disturbing thoughts   106 *peise*
weigh   111 *irons* swords   117 *windows* eyelids   122 *cheerful* full of joy
125 *anointed* (see IV, i, 61n.)

By thee was punchèd full of deadly holes.
Think on the Tower, and me : despair, and die !
Harry the Sixth bids thee despair, and die !
   (To Richmond)
Virtuous and holy, be thou conqueror !
Harry, that prophesied thou shouldst be king,
Doth comfort thee in thy sleep : live, and flourish !
   Enter the Ghost of Clarence.
GHOST *[to Richard]*
Let me sit heavy in thy soul to-morrow –
I that was washed to death with fulsome wine,   133
Poor Clarence by thy guile betrayed to death !
To-morrow in the battle think on me,
And fall thy edgeless sword : despair, and die !   136
   (To Richmond)
Thou offspring of the house of Lancaster,   137
The wrongèd heirs of York do pray for thee ;
Good angels guard thy battle ! live, and flourish !
   Enter the Ghosts of Rivers, Grey, and Vaughan.
RIVERS *[to Richard]*
Let me sit heavy in thy soul to-morrow,
Rivers, that died at Pomfret ! despair, and die !
GREY
Think upon Grey, and let thy soul despair !
VAUGHAN
Think upon Vaughan, and with guilty fear
Let fall thy lance : despair, and die !
ALL *(to Richmond)*
Awake, and think our wrongs in Richard's bosom
Will conquer him ! Awake, and win the day !

---

133 *fulsome* sickening or satiating   **136** *fall . . . sword* i.e. let thy sword,
figuratively blunted by thinking about Clarence's murder, drop (1) out of
your hand, or (2) down, so that it is no longer a means of defense   **137**
offspring . . . Lancaster (Richmond's mother was a Beaufort and the Beaufort
line traced back to John of Gaunt, Duke of Lancaster, the father of Boling-
broke, who became Henry IV)

Enter the Ghost of Lord Hastings.

GHOST *[to Richard]*
Bloody and guilty, guiltily awake
And in a bloody battle end thy days!
Think on Lord Hastings: despair, and die!
(To Richmond)
150   Quiet untroublèd soul, awake, awake!
Arm, fight, and conquer, for fair England's sake!
Enter the Ghosts of the two young Princes.

GHOSTS *[to Richard]*
Dream on thy cousins smotherèd in the Tower.
Let us be lead within thy bosom, Richard,
And weigh thee down to ruin, shame, and death!
Thy nephews' souls bid thee despair, and die!
(To Richmond)
Sleep, Richmond, sleep in peace and wake in joy.
157   Good angels guard thee from the boar's annoy!
Live, and beget a happy race of kings!
Edward's unhappy sons do bid thee flourish.
Enter the Ghost of Anne, his wife.

GHOST *(to Richard)*
Richard, thy wife, that wretched Anne thy wife,
That never slept a quiet hour with thee,
Now fills thy sleep with perturbations:
To-morrow in the battle think on me,
And fall thy edgeless sword: despair, and die!
(To Richmond)
Thou quiet soul, sleep thou a quiet sleep.
Dream of success and happy victory!
Thy adversary's wife doth pray for thee.
Enter the Ghost of Buckingham.

GHOST *(to Richard)*
The first was I that helped thee to the crown;
The last was I that felt thy tyranny.

157 *annoy* molestation

O, in the battle think on Buckingham,
And die in terror of thy guiltiness !
Dream on, dream on, of bloody deeds and death :
Fainting, despair ; despairing, yield thy breath !
(To Richmond)
I died for hope ere I could lend thee aid ;   174
But cheer thy heart and be thou not dismayed :
God and good angels fight on Richmond's side,
And Richard falls in height of all his pride !
[The Ghosts vanish.] Richard starts out of his dream.

KING RICHARD

Give me another horse ! Bind up my wounds !
Have mercy, Jesu ! Soft ! I did but dream.
O coward conscience, how dost thou afflict me !
The lights burn blue. It is now dead midnight.
Cold fearful drops stand on my trembling flesh.
What do I fear ? Myself ? There's none else by.
Richard loves Richard : that is, I am I.   184
Is there a murderer here ? No. Yes, I am :
Then fly. What, from myself ? Great reason why —
Lest I revenge. What, myself upon myself ?
Alack, I love myself. Wherefore ? For any good
That I myself have done unto myself ?
O no ! Alas, I rather hate myself
For hateful deeds committed by myself.
I am a villain. Yet I lie, I am not.
Fool, of thyself speak well. Fool, do not flatter.
My conscience hath a thousand several tongues,   194
And every tongue brings in a several tale,
And every tale condemns me for a villain.
Perjury, perjury, in the highest degree,
Murder, stern murder, in the direst degree,

174 *for hope* for the intent (of helping) (?)   184 *I am I* (this reading, that of
all texts except Quarto 1, has the sanction of all later editors, but the reading
'I and I' of Quarto 1, here admittedly the basic text, makes equally good
sense)   194 *several* separate

199   All several sins, all used in each degree,
       Throng to the bar, crying all, 'Guilty! guilty!'
       I shall despair. There is no creature loves me ;
       And if I die, no soul will pity me.
       And, wherefore should they, since that I myself
       Find in myself no pity to myself ?
       Methought the souls of all that I had murdered
       Came to my tent, and every one did threat
       To-morrow's vengeance on the head of Richard.
                    Enter Ratcliffe.

RATCLIFFE
   My lord !
KING RICHARD
   Zounds, who is there ?
RATCLIFFE
210   Ratcliffe, my lord, 'tis I. The early village cock
       Hath twice done salutation to the morn :
       Your friends are up and buckle on their armor.
[KING RICHARD
   O Ratcliffe, I have dreamed a fearful dream !
   What think'st thou ? Will our friends prove all true ?
RATCLIFFE
   No doubt, my lord.]
KING RICHARD   O Ratcliffe, I fear, I fear !
RATCLIFFE
   Nay, good my lord, be not afraid of shadows.
KING RICHARD
   By the apostle Paul, shadows to-night
   Have struck more terror to the soul of Richard
   Than can the substance of ten thousand soldiers
   Armèd in proof and led by shallow Richmond.
   'Tis not yet near day. Come, go with me.
222   Under our tents I'll play the easedropper,
       To see if any mean to shrink from me.
                    Exeunt Richard and Ratcliffe.

---

199 *All . . . degree* all kinds of sins, each one practised in all its comparative
stages (e.g. bad, worse, worst ; cf. ll. 197–98)   222 *easedropper* eavesdropper

Enter the Lords to Richmond sitting in his tent.

LORDS

Good morrow, Richmond.

RICHMOND

Cry mercy, lords and watchful gentlemen,   225
That you have ta'en a tardy sluggard here.

LORDS

How have you slept, my lord?

RICHMOND

The sweetest sleep, and fairest-boding dreams   228
That ever ent'red in a drowsy head
Have I since your departure had, my lords.
Methought their souls whose bodies Richard murdered
Came to my tent and cried on victory.   232
I promise you my soul is very jocund   233
In the remembrance of so fair a dream.
How far into the morning is it, lords?

LORDS

Upon the stroke of four.

RICHMOND

Why, then 'tis time to arm and give direction.
          His Oration to his Soldiers.
More than I have said, loving countrymen,
The leisure and enforcement of the time   239
Forbids to dwell upon. Yet remember this:
God and our good cause fight upon our side;
The prayers of holy saints and wrongèd souls,
Like high-reared bulwarks, stand before our faces.   243
Richard except, those whom we fight against
Had rather have us win than him they follow.
For what is he they follow? Truly, gentlemen,
A bloody tyrant and a homicide;

225 *Cry mercy* beg pardon   228 *fairest-boding* most propitious   232 *cried on* urged (me) on to   233 *jocund* joyful   239 *leisure* (see l. 98)   243 *bulwarks* defensive ramparts

248   One raised in blood and one in blood established;
249   One that made means to come by what he hath,
       And slaughtered those that were the means to help him;
251   A base foul stone, made precious by the foil
       Of England's chair, where he is falsely set;
       One that hath ever been God's enemy.
       Then if you fight against God's enemy,
255   God will in justice ward you as his soldiers;
       If you do sweat to put a tyrant down,
       You sleep in peace, the tyrant being slain;
       If you do fight against your country's foes,
259   Your country's fat shall pay your pains the hire;
       If you do fight in safeguard of your wives,
       Your wives shall welcome home the conquerors;
       If you do free your children from the sword,
263   Your children's children quits it in your age:
       Then in the name of God and all these rights,
       Advance your standards, draw your willing swords.
266   For me, the ransom of my bold attempt
       Shall be this cold corpse on the earth's cold face;
       But if I thrive, the gain of my attempt
       The least of you shall share his part thereof.
       Sound drums and trumpets boldly and cheerfully:
       God and Saint George! Richmond and victory!

[Exeunt.]
Enter King Richard, Ratcliffe [and Soldiers].

KING RICHARD
   What said Northumberland as touching Richmond?

---

248 *One . . . established* i.e. one who came to the throne through bloodshed and has held it through further bloodshed (this is the theme of Richmond's justification for deposing Richard)   **249** *One . . . means* i.e. one who did not let events take their natural course but engineered them to his advantage **251** *foil* metal leaf (*England's chair* or throne) placed under a jewel (Richard) to make it appear more brilliant than it is   **255** *ward* protect   **259** *fat* abundant fertility   **263** *quits* requites   **266–67** *the ransom . . . face* i.e. (if we fail) my only ransom (freeing from captivity) will be by death

RATCLIFFE
  That he was never trainèd up in arms.
KING RICHARD
  He said the truth. And what said Surrey then?
RATCLIFFE
  He smiled and said, 'The better for our purpose.'
KING RICHARD
  He was in the right, and so indeed it is.
        Clock strikes.
  Tell the clock there. Give me a calendar.   277
  Who saw the sun to-day?
RATCLIFFE   Not I, my lord.
KING RICHARD
  Then he disdains to shine; for by the book
  He should have braved the East an hour ago.
  A black day will it be to somebody.
  Ratcliffe!
RATCLIFFE
  My lord?
KING RICHARD The sun will not be seen to-day;
  The sky doth frown and low'r upon our army.
  I would these dewy tears were from the ground.   285
  Not shine to-day? Why, what is that to me
  More than to Richmond? For the selfsame heaven
  That frowns on me looks sadly upon him.
        Enter Norfolk.
NORFOLK
  Arm, arm, my lord; the foe vaunts in the field.
KING RICHARD
  Come, bustle, bustle! Caparison my horse!   290
  Call up Lord Stanley, bid him bring his power.
  I will lead forth my soldiers to the plain,
  And thus my battle shall be orderèd:
  My foreward shall be drawn out all in length,
  Consisting equally of horse and foot;

277 *calendar* almanac   285 *dewy tears* i.e. morning dew ('tears' because the
sky frowns, l. 284)   290 *Caparison* cover with a rich horse-cloth

Our archers shall be placèd in the midst;
John Duke of Norfolk, Thomas Earl of Surrey,
Shall have the leading of this foot and horse.
299 They thus directed, we will follow
300 In the main battle, whose puissance on either side
301 Shall be well wingèd with our chiefest horse.
302 This, and Saint George to boot! What think'st thou,
        Norfolk?

NORFOLK
A good direction, warlike sovereign.
This found I on my tent this morning.
        [He showeth him a paper.]
305 'Jockey of Norfolk, be not so bold,
306 For Dickon thy master is bought and sold.'

KING RICHARD
A thing devisèd by the enemy.
308 Go, gentlemen, every man unto his charge.
Let not our babbling dreams affright our souls;
Conscience is but a word that cowards use,
Devised at first to keep the strong in awe:
312 Our strong arms be our conscience, swords our law!
March on, join bravely, let us to it pell-mell,
If not to heaven, then hand in hand to hell.
        [His Oration to his Army.]
315 What shall I say more than I have inferred?
316 Remember whom you are to cope withal—
317 A sort of vagabonds, rascals, and runaways,
318 A scum of Britains and base lackey peasants,
Whom their o'ercloyèd country vomits forth

---

299 *directed* placed tactically 300 *puissance* force or power 301 *well wingèd . . . horse* i.e. the best horsemen will be well deployed as wings (on either side of the main body of troops; cf. *main battle*, l. 300) 302 *to boot* as a helper 305 *Jockey* i.e. John or Jack (familiar form) 306 *Dickon* i.e. Richard or Dick (familiar form) 308–42 *Go . . . staves* (note how Shakespeare is moved imaginatively by Richard in these lines; cf. the comparative flatness of Richmond's oration, ll. 238–71) 312 *strong . . . conscience* i.e. might makes right 315 *inferred* reported 316 *cope withal* meet with 317 *sort* band 318 *Britains* Bretons; *lackey* camp-following

To desperate adventures and assured destruction.
You sleeping safe, they bring to you unrest;
You having lands, and blessed with beauteous wives,
They would restrain the one, distain the other.   323
And who doth lead them but a paltry fellow,
Long kept in Britain at our mother's cost,   325
A milksop, one that never in his life
Felt so much cold as over shoes in snow?   327
Let's whip these stragglers o'er the seas again,
Lash hence these overweening rags of France,
These famished beggars, weary of their lives,
Who (but for dreaming on this fond exploit)   331
For want of means (poor rats) had hanged themselves.   332
If we be conquered, let men conquer us,
And not these bastard Britains, whom our fathers
Have in their own land beaten, bobbed, and thumped,
And, in record, left them the heirs of shame.
Shall these enjoy our lands? lie with our wives?
Ravish our daughters?
    Drum afar off.   Hark! I hear their drum.
Fight, gentlemen of England! Fight, bold yeomen!
Draw, archers, draw your arrows to the head!
Spur your proud horses hard, and ride in blood!   341
Amaze the welkin with your broken staves!   342
    Enter a Messenger.
What says Lord Stanley? Will he bring his power?

MESSENGER
My lord, he doth deny to come.

KING RICHARD
Off with his son George's head!

NORFOLK
My lord, the enemy is past the marsh:

---

323 *restrain* deprive you of; *distain* dishonor, sully   325 *Britain* Brittany
327 *over . . . snow* i.e. snow deeper than shoe level   331 *but for* if it were not
for; *fond* foolish   332 *means* the wherewithal to live   341 *in blood* (1) in full
vigor (a hunting term), (2) smeared with blood from spurring   342 *welkin*
sky; *staves* lance shafts

    After the battle let George Stanley die.

KING RICHARD
    A thousand hearts are great within my bosom!
    Advance our standards, set upon our foes.
350   Our ancient word of courage, fair Saint George,
351   Inspire us with the spleen of fiery dragons!
    Upon them! Victory sits on our helms.   *[Exeunt.]*

*

V, iv   *Alarum; excursions. Enter [Norfolk and Forces;
        to him] Catesby.*

    CATESBY
    Rescue, my Lord of Norfolk, rescue, rescue!
    The king enacts more wonders than a man,
3   Daring an opposite to every danger:
    His horse is slain, and all on foot he fights,
    Seeking for Richmond in the throat of death.
    Rescue, fair lord, or else the day is lost!
      Alarums. Enter [King] Richard.

    KING RICHARD
7   A horse! a horse! my kingdom for a horse!
    CATESBY
    Withdraw, my lord; I'll help you to a horse.
    KING RICHARD
9   Slave, I have set my life upon a cast,
10   And I will stand the hazard of the die.
11   I think there be six Richmonds in the field;
    Five have I slain to-day instead of him.
    A horse! a horse! my kingdom for a horse!   *[Exeunt.]*

---

350 *word* battle cry   **351** *spleen* fiery temper
V, iv The same   **3** *Daring an opposite* offering himself as an opponent   **7** *A
horse . . . horse* (cf. *The True Tragedie of Richard III :* 'A horse, a horse, a
fresh horse.' It seems likely that Shakespeare derived his famous line from
this rather flat hint.)   **9** *cast* throw (of the dice)   **10** *die* (singular of dice)
11 *six Richmonds* i.e. in addition to Richmond, five other men dressed and
armed to resemble Richmond (a common safety measure)

R dead

Alarum. Enter [King] Richard and Richmond; they　　**V, v**
fight; Richard is slain. Retreat and flourish.
Enter Richmond, [Lord Stanley Earl of] Derby,
bearing the crown, with divers other Lords.

RICHMOND

God and your arms be praised, victorious friends!
The day is ours; the bloody dog is dead.

DERBY

Courageous Richmond, well hast thou acquit thee.
Lo, here this long usurpèd royalty
From the dead temples of this bloody wretch
Have I plucked off, to grace thy brows withal.
Wear it, enjoy it, and make much of it.

RICHMOND

Great God of heaven, say amen to all!
But tell me, is young George Stanley living?

DERBY

He is, my lord, and safe in Leicester town,
Whither, if it please you, we may now withdraw us.

RICHMOND

What men of name are slain on either side?

DERBY

John Duke of Norfolk, Walter Lord Ferrers,
Sir Robert Brakenbury, and Sir William Brandon.

RICHMOND

Inter their bodies as become their births.
Proclaim a pardon to the soldiers fled
That in submission will return to us;
And then, as we have ta'en the sacrament,　　　　18
We will unite the White Rose and the Red.　　　　19

V, v   s.d. *Retreat* a trumpet signal for Richard's men to retire   18 *as
. . . sacrament* (referring to the oath, taken by Richmond in the cathedral
at Rheims, that he would marry Princess Elizabeth as soon as he was
possessed of the crown)   19 *White Rose . . . Red* i.e. the badges of the
Yorkist and Lancastrian factions respectively; the marriage of Richmond
(Lancastrian) and Princess Elizabeth (Yorkist) will bring an end to the
so-called Wars of the Roses (see ll. 27–31)

20   Smile heaven upon this fair conjunction,
        That long have frowned upon their enmity!
        What traitor hears me, and says not amen?
        England hath long been mad and scarred herself;
        The brother blindly shed the brother's blood;
25   The father rashly slaughtered his own son;
        The son, compelled, been butcher to the sire:
        All this divided York and Lancaster,
        Divided in their dire division,
        O, now let Richmond and Elizabeth,
        The true succeeders of each royal house,
        By God's fair ordinance conjoin together!
        And let their heirs (God, if thy will be so)
        Enrich the time to come with smooth-faced peace,
        With smiling plenty, and fair prosperous days!
35   Abate the edge of traitors, gracious Lord,
36   That would reduce these bloody days again
        And make poor England weep in streams of blood!
        Let them not live to taste this land's increase
        That would with treason wound this fair land's peace!
        Now civil wounds are stopped, peace lives again:
        That she may long live here, God say amen!

                                        Exeunt.

20 *conjunction* marriage union (with play on the astrological meaning: the Sun [the king symbol: Richmond] and Venus [Elizabeth] will be 'in conjunction,' i.e. in the same sign of the zodiac at the same time)   25–26 *The father . . . sire* (Shakespeare seems to be recalling *3 Henry VI*, II, v)   35 *Abate the edge* i.e. blunt the sharpness (of traitors' swords)   36 *reduce* bring back

APPENDIX:
THE QUARTO AND FOLIO TEXTS

As pointed out in the "Note on the text," the textual problems involved in *Richard III* are extremely complex and no completely satisfactory agreement among textual critics has yet been reached. The fact that the greater part of the first folio (1623) text is probably printed from a copy of Quarto 6 (1622) which had been corrected against a manuscript (possibly Shakespeare's autograph or a "fair copy" of Shakespeare's autograph) opens the way to many possibilities of corruption. First, the person (or persons) responsible for collating the manuscript with Quarto 6 seems to have been erratic in the care with which he executed his task. Second, two substantial stretches of text (III, i, 1–158, and V, iii, 48 to end), in all about 500 lines, appear to have been printed directly from an uncorrected copy of Quarto 3 (1602). Third, Quarto 1 (1597), from which the succeeding seven quartos derive in a mounting spiral of compositorial error and unauthoritative emendation, is generally accepted as a memorially reported text and hence of uncertain authority in all its readings. It will thus be seen that the first folio text may be considered open to question at almost every point; nevertheless, because it shows evidence of authoritative correction from a manuscript source and because it contains a substantial number of unique lines, it remains the best extant text of the play and has been used as the basis of the present edition.

In the passages unique to the first folio we come closer perhaps to Shakespeare's original and unadulterated text than in any other parts of the play. They have, therefore, a special interest. The following is a complete list of these passages (single words and phrases not included):

I, ii, 16, 25, 155–66   I, iii, 115, 166–68, 353–54 ('straight . . .

lord') I, iv, 28, 36–37 ('and . . . ghost'), 69–72, 84, 98–99 ('Fare you well'), 112–13, 129 ("'Tis no matter"), 165, 211, 252–55, 261, 263

II, i, 25, 141   II, ii, 16, 89–100, 123–40   II, iii, 6 ('Give . . . sir') II, iv, 67

III, i, 172–73   III, ii, 112, 123 ('I'll . . . lordship')   III, iii, 7–8, 16   III, iv, 102–05   III, v, 7, 97 ('and . . . adieu'), 103–05 III, vii, 5–6, 8, 11, 24 ('they . . . word'), 37, 82 ('Here . . . again'), 98–99, 120, 127, 144–53, 202, 245

IV, i, 2–6, 14 ('and . . . York'), 36, 97–103   IV, ii, 2, 41 ('I . . . man'), 45 ('Well, be it so')   IV, iii, 35 ('I . . . leave')   IV, iv, 20–21, 28, 52–53, 103, 160, 173, 180 ('Strike . . . drum'), 222–35, 276–77 ('which . . . body'), 288–342, 387 ('What . . . now'), 400, 429, 432, 443–44 ('I will . . . hither'), 452

V, iii, 27–28, 43

Stated generally, the theory on which the present text has been constructed is as follows. Taking the first folio text as a basis, the readings of the folio text have been preferred to those of the quarto texts (in most cases only Quarto 1 is concerned) except (1) where the folio text follows readings of Quartos 2–6 in preference to the reading of Quarto 1 (the inference is that, since the readings of the later quartos are without authority, the corrector of the copy for the first folio, working probably for the most part with a copy of Quarto 6, has failed to correct his text at these points and that we, therefore, approach more nearly to Shakespeare's original by reverting to Quarto 1); (2) where the folio text (at III, i, 1–158, and V, iii, 48 to end) is apparently printed directly from an uncorrected copy of Quarto 3, since in these passages Quarto 1, equivocal though it may be, must be considered as the basic text (the folio readings for these two sections of the text are recorded in the textual notes); (3) where the folio text omits passages or words in Quarto 1 which are so excellent that they stand on their own merits (e.g. IV, ii, 97–115) or are necessary for the meaning (the additional passages supplied from Quarto 1 have been placed in square brackets and are not otherwise recorded in the textual notes, whereas additions of one or two words are unbracketed but are recorded); (4) where the folio text is manifestly in error (e.g. see the textual note at II, i, 68). This is the theory, but in practice some editorial judgment in the choice of readings has still to be admitted.

In the following textual notes all significant variations from the first folio text (1623) have been recorded, but no attempt has been made to set up a complete textual apparatus in terms of the eight quarto and four folio editions. The student will find such an apparatus in either the "Cambridge Shakespeare" (1892) or the New Variorum *Richard III* (1909). The abbreviations here used are : F = the folios of 1623, 1632, 1664, 1685. Where the folios do not agree among themselves the reading of F1 (= the first folio) has been given; the readings of the later folios, whether one or more may agree with F1, have not been recorded. Q = the six quartos of 1597, 1598, 1602, 1605, 1612, 1622 (the last two quartos of 1629 and 1634 are of no concern here). Where there is disagreement among the quartos the reading of Q1 (= Quarto 1) has been given, but this distinction is not intended to exclude the possible agreement of some of the remaining five quartos with Q1. In a majority of cases where a Q1 reading has been preferred to a F1 reading, the F1 reading represents a reading inherited from Quartos 2–6. QF = agreement of the first six quartos and the four folios. Eds = emendation by editors of Shakespeare from Nicholas Rowe (1709) to the present day. Significant readings in the quartos for which there is no general equivalent in the folio text and which have not otherwise been included as part of the present edition are also recorded in the textual notes.

Stage directions or parts of stage directions enclosed in square brackets have been added either from Q1 or from Rowe and later editors and are not recorded in the textual notes. In III, i, 1–158, and V, iii, 48 to end, where the copy-text is basically Q1, the stage directions of F1 have still been preferred to those of Q1, and Q1 stage directions bracketed as elsewhere. The usage of *u* and *v* has been modernized in the QF readings, and a grave accent has been added in some QF readings to clarify the pronunciation of the final -*èd*. Throughout the adopted reading is in italics.

I, i, 38 *up* (Q subs.) up : (F)   41 s.d. *Clarence guarded* (Eds) Clarence with a gard of men (Q) Clarence, and Brakenbury, guarded (F)   45 *the* (Q) th' (F)   52 *for* (Q) but (F)   64 *she* (Q subs.) shee. (F1)   65 *tempers . . . extremity* (Q1) tempts him to this harsh Extremity (F)   71 *is secure* (Eds) is securde (Q1) secure (F)   75 *Lord . . . delivery* (Q adds 'to her' after *was*)   *his* (Q) her (F1)   88 *so?* (Eds) so (Q) so, (F)   95 *gentlefolks* (Q1) gentle Folkes

(F1)   101–02 *Brakenbury. What . . . betray me?* (first appears in
Q2, 1598)   124 *the* (Q1) this (F)   133 *prey* (Q) play (F)

I, ii, 27 *life* (Eds; cf. IV, i, 75) death (QF)   39 *Stand* (Q) Stand'st
(F1)   78 *a* (Q) Omitted (F)   80 *t'accuse* (Eds) to curse (QF)
102 *hedgehog?* (Eds) hedgehogge (Q1) Hedgehogge, (F)   138
thee (Q) the (F1)   141 *He lives . . . could* (Q adds 'Go to,' before
He)   195 *was man* (Q1) man was (F)   201 *Vouchsafe . . . ring*
(given to Anne in F; here assigned as in Q)   235 *at all* (Q1)
withall (F)

I, iii, 17 *come the lords* (Q1) comes the Lord (F)   68 *he . . . ground*
(F) thereby he may gather / The ground of your ill will and to
remove it (Q1)   101 *Iwis* (Q1) I wis (F)   141 *childish-foolish*
(Eds) childish, foolish (Q1) childish foolish (F)   159 *of* (Q) off
(F1)   214 *with'red* (Q1) wither'd (F)   246 False-boding (Eds)
false boading (QF)   287 *gentle-sleeping* (Eds) gentle sleeping
(QF)   303 *Buckingham* (F) Hast. (Q)   308 *Queen Elizabeth*
(Eds) Qu. (Q1) Hast. (Q6) Mar. (F1)   341, 349 *1. Murderer* (Eds)
Execu. (Q) Vil. (F)   343 *Well . . . about me* (Q precedes *Well*
with 'It was')   350 *doers. Be* (F4) doers be (Q1) dooers, be (F1)
354 *1. Murderer* (Eds) Vil. (F) Speech omitted (Q)

I, iv, s.d. *Keeper* (Keeper's role is given to Brakenbury in Q)
13 *thence* (Q1) there (F)   22 *waters* (Q1) water (F)   48 *stranger
soul* (Q) Stranger-soule (F)   58 *methoughts* (Q1) me thought (F)
68 *requites* (Q) requits (F1)   86 *1. Murderer* (Eds) Execu. (Q)
2. Mur. (F)   89 *2. Murderer* (Eds) 2 Exe. (Q) 1. (F)   100 *I* (Q1)
we (F)   103 *Why, he* (Q reads 'When he wakes, / Why foole
he')   110–11 *warrant can* (Q adds 'for it' after *warrant*)   120
Faith (Q) Omitted (F)   124 *Zounds* (Q) Come (F)   131 *I'll
not . . . with it* (Q adds 'it is a dangerous thing' after *it*)   138
It is turned . . . towns (Q adds 'all' before *towns*)   141 *Zounds*
(Q) Omitted (F)   146 *I am strong-framed* (Q adds 'Tut' before
I am)   *strong-framed* (Eds) strong in fraud (Q) strong fram'd
(F)   146 *he cannot prevail . . . me* (Q adds 'I warrant thee'
after *me*)   153–54 *Soft! . . . Strike!* (Q reads '1 Harke he stirs,
shall I strike.')   166 *Who . . . come* (Q reads 'Tell me who
are you, wherefore come you thither)   167 *Both* (Eds) Am.
(Q) 2 (F)   184–85 *to have . . . sins* (Q) for any goodnesse (F)
208 *He sends . . . this* (Q) adds 'Why sirs' before *He*)   216
gallant-springing (Eds) gallant springing (QF)   221 *O, if you*
(Q) If you do (F)   234 *of* (Q) on (F)   235 *lessoned* (Q1) lessonèd
(F)   261 *As . . . distress* (after l. 255 in F; omitted in Q)   265

drown . . . within (Q reads 'chop thee in the malmesey But, in the next roome') 270 *heavens* (Q1) Heaven (F)

II, i, s.d. (F adds 'Woodvill' in repetition of *Rivers*) 5 *in* (Q) to (F) 7 *Hastings and Rivers* (Eds) Rivers and Hastings (Q) Dorset and Rivers (F) 28 *And so swear I* (Q adds 'my Lord' after *I*) 39 *God* (Q) heaven (F) 46 *comes . . . duke* (Q reads 'comes the noble Duke') 52 *wrong-incensèd* (Eds) wrong insencèd (QF) 57 *unwittingly* (Q) unwillingly (F; i.e. unintentionally, possibly the true reading) 59 *By* (Q) To (F) 68 *That, all . . . frowned on me* (F follows this line with 'Of you Lord Woodvill, and Lord Scales of you'; both names are titles of Rivers, already referred to in l. 67) 82 *King Edward* (F) Ryv. (Q) 93 *but* (Q) and (F) 108 *at* (Q) and (F1) 117 *Even . . . give himself* (Q1 adds 'owne' before *garments*)

II, ii, 1 *Boy* (Q) Edw. (F) 3 *Girl* (Eds) Daugh. (F; throughout) Boy (Q) 47 *I* (Q) Omitted (F) 83 *weep* (Q) weepes (F1) 86 *distressed,* (Q1) distrest: (F1) 112 *cloudy princes* (Q) clowdy-Princes (F) *heart-sorrowing peers* (Q1) hart-sorrowing-Peeres (F) 142, 154 *Ludlow* (Q) London (F) 144 *To give . . . business* (Q adds 'waighty' before *business*) 145 *Both* (Eds) Ans. (Q; speech omitted in F)

II, iii, 8 *Ay, sir . . . true* (Q reads '1 It doth.') 32 *wise men* (Q) wisemen (F1) 43 *Ensuing* (Q) Pursuing (F; catchword 'Ensuing' in F1)

II, iv, 1 *hear* (Q1) heard (F) 21 *Archbishop* (Eds) Car. (Q) Yor. (F) 38 *Here . . . news?* (Q reads 'Here comes your sonne, Lo: M. Dorset. / What newes Lo: Marques?') 65 *death* (Q) earth (F)

III, i, 8 *dived* (F) divèd (Q) 9 *Nor* (Q) No (F) 40 *God in heaven* (Q1) God (F) 43 *deep* (Q1) great (F) 44 *senseless-obstinate* (Eds) sencelesse obstinate (QF) 51 *claimed . . . deserved* (F) claimèd . . . deservèd (Q) 56 *never* (Q) ne're (F) 57 *overrule* (Q) o're-rule (F) 60 s.d. *Exeunt* (Eds) Exit (Q3, F) 63 *seems* (Q1) thinkst (F) 71 *since, succeeding* (F) since succeeding (Q) 78 *all-ending* (Q1) ending (F) 82 *Vice, Iniquity* (F) vice iniquity (Q1) 86 *valor* (F) valure (Q1) 87 *this* (Q1) his (F) 96 *loving* (Q1) noble (F) 97 *dread* (Q1) deare (F) 98 *brother – to* (Eds) brother to (Q1) brother, to (F) 111 *With all* (F) withall (Q1) 120 *heavy* (Q1) weightie (F) 123 *as* (Q1) as, as (F1) 132 *sharp-provided* (Eds) sharpe provided (QF) 133–34 *uncle, . . . himself:* (F) Unckle: . . . himselfe, (Q1) 141 *needs* (Q1) Omitted (F) 145 *grandam* (F) Granam (Q) *murd'red* (Q) murther'd (F)

149 *with* (Q) and with (F)   150 s.d. *Hastings* (Eds) Hast. Dors.
(Q) Hastings, and Dorset (F; Dorset has not been present in the
scene)   s.d. *Manent* (F2) manet (Q, FI)   171–74 *purpose . . .
us* (Q reads 'purpose, if he be willing')

III, ii, 2 *Who knocks* (Q adds 'at the dore' after *knocks*)   3 s.d.
Enter Lord Hastings (after l. 5 in F)   41 *How! . . . garland!*
(Eds) Howe? . . . garland? (Q1) How . . . Garland? (F)   *Dost*
(F3) Doest (Q, FI)   60 *Well . . . older* (Q reads 'I tell thee
Catesby. *Cat.* What my Lord? / *Hast.* Ere a fortnight make me

III, iv, 10 *We know . . . hearts* (In Q Buckingham precedes this line
with 'Who I my Lo?')   31 *My . . . when* (Q reads '*Hast.* I
thanke your Grace. / *Glo.* My Lo : of Elie, *Bish.* My Lo : / *Glo.*
When)   34 *Marry . . . heart* (Q reads 'I go my Lord')   79 s.d.
Manent (F2) manet (Q, FI)   82 *rase* (Q) rowse (F)   *our helms* (F)
his helme (Q; perhaps correctly)   83 *But* (Q) And (F)
elder')   78 *you do* (Q) Omitted (F)   89–91 *What . . . lords* (Q
reads 'But come my Lo : shall we to the tower? *Hast.* I go : but
stay, heare you not the newes, / This day those men')   91
talked (Q1) talke (F)   95 *Go . . . fellow* (Q reads 'Go you before,
Ile follow presently')   s.d. *Exeunt* (Eds) Exit (Q3, F)   96 *How
now, sirrah* (Q reads 'Well met Hastings')   108–09 *Priest. Well
. . . heart* (Q reads '*Hast.* What Sir Iohn, you are wel met')

III, v, 5 *Tut . . . tragedian* (Q adds 'feare not me' after *Tut*)   12–14
But . . . Mayor – (Q reads '*Glo.* Here comes the Maior. / *Buc.*
Let me alone to entertaine him. Lo : Maior,')   20 *innocence*
(Q1) Innocencie (F)   21 *Be . . . Lovel.* (Q reads 'O, O, be quiet,
it is Catesby.' with Lovel's following speech given to Catesby)
34 *Look . . . Mayor* (from Q, where it follows l. 26)   50–51 *I
never . . . Shore* (assigned to Mayor in Q)   66 *cause* (Q1) case (F)
74 *meet'st advantage* (Q1) meetest vantage (F)   102 *Look for . . .
affords* (Q adds 'and so my Lord farewell' after *affords*)   104
Penker (Eds) Peuker (F1) Omitted (Q)   105 s.d. *Exeunt* (Eds)
Exit (F, Omitted Q)   109 s.d. *Exit* (Q) Exeunt (F1)

III, vi, 12 *who's* (Q1) who (F)

III, vii, 20 *mine* (Q1) my (F)   *to an* (Q1) toward (F)   33 *spake* (Q1)
spoke (F)   40 *wisdoms* (Q1) wisdome (F)   52 *I . . . plead* (Q reads
'Feare not me, if thou canst pleade')   55–56 *Go . . . lord* (Q
reads 'You shal see what I can do, get you up to the leads.
Exit. / Now my L. Maior,')   58 *Now . . . request?* (Q reads
'Here coms his servant : how now Catesby what saies he.')   83
My lord (Q) Omitted (F)   125 *her* (Q1) his (F)   126 *Her* (Q) His

(F) 127 *Her* (Eds) His (F; line omitted in Q) 131–32 *charge
. . . land* (Q reads 'soveraingtie thereof') 219 *Zounds, I'll* (Q) we
will (F) 222 *If . . . it* (Q reads '*Ano*. Doe, good my lord, least all
the land do rew it) 247 *cousin* (Q) Cousins (F)

IV, i, 2–7 *Led . . . away* (Q reads 'Sister well met, whether awaie so
fast') 14 *How . . . York* (Q reads 'How fares the Prince') 16
them (F) him (Q) 18 *The king . . . Protector* (Q adds 'I cric you
mercie' before *mean*) 28 *an* (Q1) one (F) 30 *looker-on* (Eds)
looker on (QF)

IV, ii, 13 *liege* (Q) Lord (F) 36 *I know . . . gentleman* (Q precedes
this line with 'My lord') 42 *deep-revolving* (Eds) deepe revolving (QF) 48 *To Richmond . . . abides* (Q adds 'beyond the
seas' after *parts*) 49 *Come hither, Catesby.* (Q reads 'Catesby.
Cat. My lord.') 71 *there* (Q) then (F) 81 *I . . . straight* (Q1 reads
'Tis done my gracious lord. / *King* Shal we heare from thee
Tirrel ere we sleep? / *Tir.* Ye shall my lord' – apparently a
memorial slip repeating III, i, 188–89) 89 *Hereford* (F2) Her-
ford (Q) Hertford (F1) 104 *called* (Eds) callèd (Q) 116–17
May . . . Thou (Q reads 'Whie then resolve me whether you wil
or no? / *King*. Tut, tut, thou') 117 s.d. *Exeunt* (Eds) Exit (QF)

IV, iii, 5 *ruthless* (Q1) ruthfull (F) 7 *kind* (Q1) milde (F) 8 *to* (F)
two (Q) 13 *Which* (Q1) And (F) 15 *once* (Q) one (F) 27 *For it
is done* (Q adds 'my Lord' after *done*) 31 *at* (Q) and (F) 33
thee (Q) the (F1) 50 *rash-levied* (Eds) rash levied (QF) 53
leads (Q) leds (F1)

IV, iv, 10 *unblown* (Q) unblowed (F1) *new-appearing* (Eds) new
appearing (QF) 17–19 *Duchess of York. So . . . dead?* (after l. 34
in Q) 26 *mortal-living* (Eds) mortal living (QF) 41 *Harry*
(Eds) Richard (Q) Husband (F) 45 *holp'st* (Q3) hopst (Q1, F1)
52 *That excellent . . . earth* (follows l. 53 in F; both lines omitted
in Q) 64 *Thy* (Q) The (F) 70 *smoth'red* (Q1) smother'd (F)
86 *a-high* (Eds) a high (QF) 100–01 *For one . . . with care* (Q
reverses order of lines) 103 *feared* (Eds) fearèd (F) 112
weary (Q1) wearied (F) 118 *nights . . . days* (Q1) night . . . day
(F) 128 *intestate* (Q) intestine (F) 132 *so, then* (Q) so then,
(F1) 141 *Where* (Q) Where't (F) 147–48 *Where . . . Hastings*
(Q reads 'Where is kind Hastings, Rivers, Vaughan, Gray')
180–81 *I prithee . . . bitterly* (Q reads 'O heare me speake for I
shal never see thee more. / *King.* Come, come, you are too
bitter') 200 *moe* (Q1) more (F) 239 *or* (Q1) and (F) 241 *discovered* (Q1) discoverèd (F) 266 *should be else* (Q1) else should

bee (F) 268 *would I* (Q1) I would (F) 274 *sometimes* (Q1)
sometime (F) 276 *handkercher* (Q1) hand-kercheefe (F) 284
is (Q) Omitted (F1) 324 *Of ten times* (Eds) Of ten-times (F1)
Often-times (F2) 344 *still-lasting* (Eds) still lasting (QF) 365
Harp . . . break (follows l. 363 in F; order here from Q1) 368
swear – (Eds) sweare by nothing. (Q) sweare. (F) 377 *God* – /
God's (Q) Heaven. / Heanens (F) 392 *in* (Q1) with (F) 396
o'erpast (Q) repast (F) 417 *peevish-fond* (Eds) peevish, fond
(Q1) peevish found (F) 431 *shallow, changing* (Eds) shallow
changing (Q) shallow-changing (F) s.d. *Enter Ratcliffe* (as in Q,
which omits l. 432; comes after l. 432 in F) 444 *Ratcliffe* (Eds)
Catesby (F) Omitted (Q) 457 *None good,* (F4) None good (Q)
None, good (F1) 494 *Go then . . . behind* (Q adds 'heare you' after
But) 507 *you* (Q1) ye (F) 509–10 *The news . . . waters* (Q reads
'Your grace mistakes, the newes I bring is good, / My newes is
that by sudden floud, and fall of water') 513–14 *I cry . . .
thine* (Q reads 'O I crie you mercie, I did mistake, / Ratcliffe
reward him, for the blow I gave him') 534 *tidings* (Q1) Newes
(F)

IV, v, 10 *Ha'rford-West* (Q) Hertford West (F)

V, i, 11 *my lord* (Q) Omitted (F)

V, iii, 2 *My Lord of Surrey* (Q reads 'Whie, how now Catesbie'
with next speech-prefix *'Cat,'*) 4 *My . . . liege* (Q reads 'Nor-
ffolke, come hether') 28 *you* (F2) your (F1) 46 *In to* (Q1)
Into (F) 48 *nine* (F) sixe (Q) 54 *sentinels* (F) centinell (Q) 58
Catesby (Q) Ratcliffe (F) 59 *Catesby* (Eds) Rat. (QF) 61 *sunrising* (F) sun rising (Q1) 65–66 *heavy. / Ratcliffe* (F) heavy
Ratcliffe (Q1) 68 *thou* (Q) Omitted (F) 80 *sit* (F) set (Q1) 83
loving (Q1) Noble (F)· 86 *that. The* (F) that the (Q1) 90 *the*
(Q) th' (F) 91 *mortal-staring* (Eds) mortal staring (QF) 101
sund'red (F) sundried (Q1) 102 *rites* (F) rights (Q) 105
thoughts (Q) noise (F) 113 *The* (Q) Th' (F) 115 *the* (Q1) thy
(F) 123 *butcherèd* (Q1) butcher'd (F) 126 *deadly* (Q1) Omitted
(F) 127 *me : despair* (F) me despaire (Q1) 131 *thy* (Q) Omitted (F) *sleep : live* (F) sleepe live (Q1) 132 *sit* (F) set (Q1)
146 *Will* (F) Wel (Q1) 151 s.d. *Enter . . . young Princes* (in Q1
the ghosts of the two young princes precede the ghost of
Hastings; the F order is that of the time of their deaths, as in
Q3) 155 *souls bid* (Q) soule bids (F1) 162 *perturbations* (F) pre-
turbations (Q1) 177 *falls* (Q) fall (F) 181 *now* (Q1) not (F)
183 *What . . . fear? Myself?* (Q1) What? . . . feare my Selfe? (F)

184 *am* (F) and (Q1)   186 *reason why* – (Eds) reason whie (Q1)
reason: why? (F)   197 *perjury* (Q1) Omitted (F)   *highest* (Q)
high'st (F)   198 *direst* (Q) dyr'st (F)   200 *Throng* (Q1) Throng
all (F)   *the* (Q) th' (F)   202 *will* (Q1) shall (F)   203 *And* (Q)
Nay (F)   209 *Zounds, who is* (Q) Who's (F)   223 *see* (Q1) heare
(F)   228 *fairest-boding* (Eds) fairest boding (QF)   233 *soul* (Q)
Heart (F)   243 *high-reared* (Eds) high reard (QF)   244 *Richard
except,* (Q3) Richard, except (Q1) (Richard except) (F)   248 *established* (F) establishèd (Q)   250 *slaughterèd* (Q) slaughter'd
(F)   251 *foil* (Q1) soile (F)   256 *sweat* (Q1) sweare (F)   271 s.d.
Ratcliffe [and Soldiers] (Eds) Rat, &c.(Q) Ratcliffe, and Catesby
(F)   275 *smiled* (F) smilèd (Q)   281–82 *somebody. | Ratcliffe!*
(F1) some bodie Rat. (Q)   293 *orderèd* (Q) ordred (F1)   294
out all (Q1) Omitted (F)   298 *this* (Q1) the (F)   301 *well wingèd*
(Q) well-wingèd (F1)   302 *boot* (F) bootes (Q1)   308 *unto* (Q)
to (F)   310 *Conscience is but* (Q1) For Conscience is (F)   312
conscience, swords (F) conscience swords, (Q1)   313 *to it* (Q)
too't (F)   321 *to you* (Q1) you to (F)   322 *wives* (F) wifes (Q1)
326 *milksop* (F) milkesopt (Q1)   336 *in* (Q1) on (F)   339 *Fight*
(Q1) Right (F)   *bold* (Q1) boldly (F)   352 *them! Victory* (Eds)
them victorie (Q1) them, Victorie (F)   *helms* (Q1) helpes (F1)
V, v, 4 *this . . . royalty* (Q1) these long usurped Royalties (F)   7
enjoy it (Q1) Omitted (F)   11 *if it please . . . now* (Q) (if you
please) we may (F)   13 *Derby* (F; speech printed as s.d. in Q)
Walter Lord Ferrers (Eds) Water Lord Ferris (Q1) Walter Lord
Ferris (F)   25 *slaughtered* (Q1) slaughterèd (F1)   28 *division,*
(Eds) devision. (QF)   32 *their* (Q1) thy (F)   33 *smooth-faced*
(F1) smooth-faste (Q1)

A selection of books published by Penguin is listed on the following pages.

For a complete list of books available from Penguin in the United States, write to Dept. DG, Penguin Books, 299 Murray Hill Parkway, East Rutherford, New Jersey 07073.

For a complete list of books available from Penguin in Canada, write to Penguin Books Canada Limited, 2801 John Street, Markham, Ontario L3R 1B4.

If you live in the British Isles, write to Dept. EP, Penguin Books Ltd, Harmondsworth, Middlesex.

The Complete Pelican
SHAKESPEARE

To fill the need for a convenient and authoritative one-volume edition, the thirty-eight books in the Pelican series have been brought together.

THE COMPLETE PELICAN SHAKESPEARE includes all the material contained in the separate volumes, together with a 50,000-word General Introduction and full bibliographies. It contains the first nineteen pages of the First Folio in reduced facsimile, five new drawings, and illustrated endpapers. 9¾ × 7³⁄₁₆ inches, 1520 pages.

SHAKESPEARE

Anthony Burgess

Bare entries in parish registers, a document or two, and a few legends and contemporary references make up the known life of William Shakespeare. Anthony Burgess has clothed these attractively with an extensive knowledge of Elizabethan and Jacobean England for this elaborately illustrated biography. The characters of the men Shakespeare knew, the influence of his life on his plays, and the stirring events that must have been in the minds of author, actors, and audience are engagingly described here by a writer who sees "Will" not as an ethereal bard but as a sensitive, sensual, and shrewd man from the provinces who turned his art to fortune in the most exciting years of England's history. "It was a touch of near genius to choose Mr. Burgess to write the text for a richly illustrated life of Shakespeare, for his wonderfully well-stocked mind and essentially wayward spirit are just right for summoning up an apparition of the bard which is more convincing than most"—David Holloway, *London Daily Telegraph*. With 48 plates in color and nearly 100 black-and-white illustrations.

PLAYS BY BERNARD SHAW

ANDROCLES AND THE LION

THE APPLE CART

ARMS AND THE MAN

BACK TO METHUSELAH

CAESAR AND CLEOPATRA

CANDIDA

THE DEVIL'S DISCIPLE

THE DOCTOR'S DILEMMA

HEARTBREAK HOUSE

MAJOR BARBARA

MAN AND SUPERMAN

THE MILLIONAIRESS

PLAYS UNPLEASANT
(*Widowers' Houses, The Philanderer,
Mrs Warren's Profession*)

PYGMALION

SAINT JOAN

SELECTED ONE ACT PLAYS
(*The Shewing-up of Blanco Posnet, How He Lied to Her
Husband, O'Flaherty V.C., The Inca of Perusalem, Anna-
janska, Village Wooing, The Dark Lady of the Sonnets,
Overruled, Great Catherine, Augustus Does His Bit, The
Six of Calais*)